THE
HIGHWOOD KIDS

Book Number 1

Linda Harriman

Book Number 1. The Highwood Kids
Copyright © 2020 by Linda Harriman

Bible quotations: The New King James Version

Printed and bound in Canada by
Supreme Printing Ltd., Calgary, Alberta

ISBN
978-0-2288-1217-3 (Paperback)
978-0-2288-1218-0 (eBook)

TABLE OF CONTENTS

Our Family You Will Meet Now

This is us! The Highwood Kids!
Jacqueline Katherine;   Jeffrey James
Gwendolyn Arleen;   Alan Lorne
   Our Parents:
Ryan James: Breana Karisa: McCarthy
   Our Grandparents:
Lorne James & Ella Katherine McCarthy
Gary James & Carol Gloria Kitchener
Linda Shields (we adopted her)
Daniel James & Lily June McCarthy
(we adopted our Cousins Grandparents)
   Our Cousins:
Annette Gwendolyn;   Douglas Donald
Uncle Bryan James McCarthy (Dad's cousin)
Aunt Brenda Margaret (Mom's twin sister)
   Our Great Grandparents:
Chester Lorenzo & Mable Elizabeth (McCarthy)

1

THE COWBOY WAY

"Mrs. Jenkins, stop, stop, please, stop!" Jeff yelled in a flustered voice, staring out of the bus window.

"You're just going to get your chops busted." said Butch, looking out the window. Butch, Tom and John jumped out of their seats as soon as the bus safely parked at the edge of the road. They were behind Jeff as they bounced down the steps.

"You boys be careful now. I don't want to deliver you to the hospital." Mrs. Jenkins said as she opened the door to let those four large boys race off the bus.

"Please stay in your seats." Mrs. Jenkins said. "If those four boys cannot rescue that calf, no one can.

Gwenie, Alan and I sat in silence with all the other kids, with our noses pressed against the bus windows. We watched the performance at the fence. The calf struggled with one leg caught in the two bottom wires.

"There is my dad. Let me out please." Lorrel said as his dad was getting out of his truck, parked behind the bus.

"You and your sister are safe in here until your dad calls or waves for you." said Mrs. Jenkins.

Mr. McIntosh joined the performance going on at the fence. They untangled the calf from the barbwire but kept it held on the ground. Everyone on the fence line kept a watchful eye on its mother. Snorting and pawing the ground, a short distance away, she was bellering, answering the crying of her calf.

With a come hither wave, Mr. McIntosh called "Lorrel." All eyes were on Lorrel and Susie as they hurried to the truck after Mrs. Jenkins opened the door. Lorrel opened up the door of the truck and shortly hurried to the fence with a container of suave. It is an animal ointment that helps cuts and sores from becoming infected. Lorrel hurried to the truck box for the fence stretchers and fencing pliers, as the calf was released to its mother. Mr. McIntosh shook the four boy's hands.

Jeff led the parade back to the bus as Mr. McIntosh fastened the fence stretchers onto the top wire. He sent Lorrel, with the suave, and Susie to the truck, away from the wire in case it snapped.

"Well, that only took six minutes," said Mrs. Jenkins, "so you will not be late as we do not have to go up to the McIntosh farm. And, thank you for not getting hurt out there. I didn't want to deliver injured students home."

Jeff said, "Thank you. It had to be done. That calf

was so captured in the wire, there was no way for it to get its freedom. The barbs punctured its leg in a few places but it wasn't too bad. If we had left it, it would have gotten much worse trying to fight its way out of that impossible hold."

"Great day," said Butch. "No one got a calf's hoof in the chops, and we are not beat up with bruises. He was a big calf but with the four of us, no injuries.

"Thank you for stopping and letting us help." said Jeff. "With the rules and regulations of bus driving I don't suppose it was proper for me to stop. I only stopped to stop an uprising." laughed Mrs. Jenkins.

"My Dad reminds us often of the Code of the West. He says that being a cowboy is an attitude, a mindset, a return to simpler times. It's the smell of fresh dirt in the field or garden, of fresh grain being rolled, of new hay or grass being cut; it's a life of being a care giver to family, friends and animals. It's a life of honour, where your word or a handshake is as legal as a lawyer's contract; A reputation of an honest, caring person. That is what Dad says it takes to make a cowboy or cowgirl, and I am so sure Dad would have been so disappointed in me if I did not abide by the rules and help that animal, when I saw it in such danger." said Jeff.

"Right on! Well said!" came a choir of many voices, as Mrs. Jenkins stopped the bus.

"Good night," was called by all in the bus, answered by Bruce and his four siblings as they descended the steps.

Bruce and his siblings stopped just outside the bus. We all stood in the bus to watch a herd of deer cross the road with a coyote amongst them. The deer leaped the fence as the coyote slid under the bottom wire. Their coats were shinning in the sun which was hanging low in the sky. The fields with small patches of snow stretched to the timberland with the mountains standing behind towering over the land. We sat down as the deer disappeared into a coulee that joins the Highwood River after miles of wandering about. Mrs. Jenkins watched us in the bus mirror and put the bus in gear as soon as we were all seated again.

"Good night," was called by all when Tom and his siblings reached their gate.

"Good night," was called by all when John and his siblings reached their gate, leaving us four McCarthy kids for the last stop.

Mrs. Jenkins turned the bus into the turn-around at our home before stopping and opening the doors. "You all have a great evening,"

Jeff , Gwenie, Alan and I said, "Good night and have a great evening," as we searched the farmstead for trucks. All trucks here meant Mom and Dad were home.

"Hello" we called, entering the mud room, which was answered by Mom and Dad.

"We had to rescue a calf at Kopple's place. Mr. McIntosh stopped behind the bus and helped. He tightened the fence wires. They are all so loose and the cows don't look like they are getting too much feed.

It doesn't seem right. He is so proud of his cattle, and they are definitely not up to his standards." Jeff said.

"We will check on them for sure," Dad said as he hugged Jeff and then Gwenie who flew into his arms before Alan and me.

"The house smells so nice," said Jeff as he was the first to enter the kitchen.

"Thank you" Mom said, hugging Jeff, "how was school?"

"It is just the same as usual. I can't see why I should waste my time there when I can be helping on the farm." Jeff said as Gwenie said, "My turn" which made Mom laugh, as she released Jeff and hugged Gwenie, followed by Alan and me.

"Snack is ready," Mom said as we crawled into our stools at the counter.

'Ding' was heard and Mom went to the oven to pull out eight loaves of bread. Before she got a chance to sit down, the other oven dinged. Eight more beautiful loaves of bread sat on the counter, making the house smell like a bakery. A bakery filled with pride and love of baking. Beside the loaves of bread was the big crockpot, smelling of spices, vegetables and beef that made our mouths water in anticipation of supper.

"We have the best parents in the world," Gwenie said. "Some of the other kids just get home and change their clothes and go to do chores without a snack. They think we are the most spoiled kids in the west. I think so to."

"No," Dad said, "your Mom and I were growing up. We always had snacks after school as sometimes supper never got served till eight o'clock if we had problems with chores, but we were always well loved and fed. It is our duty to love and feed you."

"The only trouble we ever have is waiting our turn to tell you everything that happened in our day," I said laughing.

Alan said, "Yah!" making everyone laugh, as Mom put a tray with six dishes of baked apples on the counter beside the filled glasses of buttermilk.

"Heavenly Father, thank you for this bounty we are about to receive. Thank you for this beautiful day and the opportunity to help one of your creatures and a neighbour. Bless us Lord that we will follow your footsteps and do your will. Bless all our family, friends, and neighbours and loved ones. Bless this food to our bodies use in Jesus name we pray. Amen." Dad prayed.

"This is so delicious." said Alan. "Hot! Hot! Hot!"

"Yes, be careful," said Mom. "Do you want some buttermilk poured on it? It will taste great with all the cinnamon."

"Please!" every one of us said from the counter that made Mom laugh.

I am Jacqueline. I prefer to be called Jackie. I am the oldest of my four siblings. I am nearly twelve years old and I have beautiful thick hair done in a French braid, the color, a lighter auburn than Mom's. Attending my last year in elementary school, and a star of the 4-H Club, Mom says I am growing taller every day. I love the farm and I am becoming an excellent cook, like Mother. I am a great helper in the house and love working with the farm animals and my herd of cows. I started with a calf that lost her mother that I pail fed five years ago and my herd is growing. I love ever moment on horseback and love making the slippers for everyone in the house as well as the slippers needed in the cream room. Helping in the cream room to make butter, buttermilk, and different cheeses, is another of my favourites. Working in the garden and helping preserve is great fun.

Jeffrey is my oldest brother whom is two years younger than I am. He prefers to be called Jeff . At nine years old, nearly ten, he is following in Dad's footsteps. He loves the farm and all the machinery, watching carefully to learn how to operate, do maintenance, and make repairs. School work is a drag as he would rather be on the farm. He adores his 4-H calf and club. Every opportunity will find him cooking and baking. Working in the garden is a favourite pastime. He designed our tree house with the help of some library books, two years ago, and Dad, Mom, Uncle Bryan and Aunt Brenda build it, along with us six kids. His favourite days include riding, making ice cream, and licking the beater after the ice cream is made.

Gwendolyn is my younger sister. She prefers to be called Gwenie. She will be eight years old, next month. Her beautiful long golden hair that she keeps in a French braid reaches to her waist. Our farm life makes her so happy. Reading, cooking knitting, sewing and decorating the house is a real passion. She learned how to make rag rugs on the sewing machine. Days in the cream room, helping to make butter and buttermilk and cheese are her best days. Garden vegetables, fruit, and berries are preserved under her helping hands. She loves riding her horse Diamond. She is practicing to become a 4-H member, with another very spoiled calf this year again. Two years ago, she got her first calf and she loves animals. She wants to be a barrel racer.

Alan is my youngest brother and don't call him the baby of the family. He is just the youngest, so far he says. He will be six years old next month. He is a born farmer and would rather be on the farm than go to school. He is competing with Gwenie to see who makes the best rag rug for our tree house. He wishes he was nine years old so he can become a 4-H member, but he already has started his herd of cattle with a calf last year. He learned to trick ride with his new horse, Topaz. They entertain us with some new tricks and just love it. He needs to buy a special trick saddle to do a lot of the tricks. He did purchase a lariat rope and practices lassoing fence posts mostly. His friends at school has bicycles but he thinks he has more fun on Topaz. He watches every move our parents and us siblings make so he can learn to do everything perfect the first time. He is a great helper in the cream room and garden, too.

What a fantastic life we live, with our parents. Dad, Ryan James McCarthy, who is six foot two inches (one hundred and eighty-nine centimetres) tall, with reddish brown hair, short sideburns, a handlebar moustache, broad shoulders and narrow waist, a strong, kind, loving cowboy that just knows how to do everything. He has so much patience to teach us. He won all-around cowboy in his high school rodeo. He has been riding since age four Grandma Ella tells us. He took welding, mechanics, carpentry, and cooking in school, which he still excels in when he can. He is really great on ice skates, and was an excellent hockey player. He loves to cook and he enjoys helping in the garden with us.

Our Mother, Breana Katherine is beautiful, talented, smart, kind, loving, patience cowgirl, standing five feet and ten inches (one hundred eighty centimetres) tall with long auburn hair. She was rodeo queen one year and rodeo princess the next year. She was a champion barrel racer. She sold her horse when her and Dad married after college.There's nothing Mom doesn't know and she teaches us everything. Between the garden, dairy, pigs, cows, chickens, turkeys, and sheep, the farm supplies most of the food for the family. Mom teaches us the methods to preserve it. We help wrap the meat for the freezer after it is aged and cut. We dig the vegetables, wash them and help take them to the root cellar for storage. The root cellar is an underground room that is kept cool. We pick the peas and shell them. We pick the beans and snap them. We watch Mom blanch them, which is to boil them just a little and then they are dumped in ice water. They are drained and we help put them in containers and into the freezer. We help pick cucumbers and stuff them in jars after we wash them. Mom makes a special brine for them. We help pick berries to make jams and jellies. We freeze some of the berries so we can put them on our homemade ice cream. We are so lucky to help and to learn as some of our friends are not allowed in their kitchens. We have the best parents in the entire world.

"It's chore time. Thank you for snack time." Alan said as he took his dishes to the dishwasher.

"Wow, we were so busy eating, none of us told stories," Gwenie said, "Weird."

"Right," Dad said, "Snack was just too good to put our spoon down for a minute to talk."

"I will be right behind you," Mom said as she turned to the crockpot. Dad walked over to hug Mom as we hurried to the mud room to go do chores.

Happily we all walked to the feed barn where Jeff turned off the valves and unhooked the skim milk and ground grain hoses that Dad had hooked up to the empty mash tank, that morning. The paddle was stirring the mash that was ready for the sixty-four feeder pigs, the boar and six sows. Mom and Dad have everything set up to work like clockwork with the least amount of work. Alan opened the garage door and Jeff started the little tractor pulling the wagon holding the mash tank. He drove out the door and Alan closed the garage door behind him. Jeff stopped so Alan could step into the basket, on the back of the trailer, and fasten the safety door. The hose is fastened to the basket so Alan can fill the troughs as Jeff drives the tractor slowly down the lane beside the troughs. They headed to the pig barn. Gwenie and I picked up the baskets to collect the eggs, as well as buckets of feed for the laying hens. We mucked out the pen scraping the dirty straw and droppings into the grate, which dumps into the pit. We filled their water containers and feed bowls. We added fresh straw and hay to the floor of the chicken pen.

We take the eggs to the room beside the cream room where we wash them. We hold each egg up to a special light that shows us the inside. If they look perfect, we put them into cartons which we date and carry to the door of the cream room. Gwenie just waited as I took off my shoes and put on my slippers to enter the cream room, the name I called it when I was two years old. This room holds the coolers, cream separator, butter churn, cheese table, pasteurization equipment, and skim milk tank, for making mash.There is cabinets to hold the jars and equipment that is needed to make the cheese. No dust or dirt are allowed in this room. The walls are all finished in washable white panels. This barn had been designed by Mom and Dad and built by McCarthy Lumber and Construction Company just before I was born. Great Grandpa often talks about that barn had more special areas in it than a castle. A place for everything and everything in its place.

Shortly after, Mom and Dad started the dairy products, a health inspector tried to go in the cream room in his outside shoes. Mom threw him off the farm. Dad still laughs about that.

Jeff and Alan have finished feeding the pigs and put the tractor away. Jeff hooked the hoses up again and opened the valves to allow the tank to fill with ground grain and skim milk, and turned the paddle on. They then went to the turkeys and baby chicks. They were scraping the floor of the pen when we girls joined them.

"You are just in time to feed and water them." Alan said. "We will go up the stairs and drop hay through the trap doors in the loft to the mangers below for the milk cows. Well, after we muck out the milk cow stall. They must have stayed inside all day and deposited. We better get the wheelbarrow."

Everyone giggled as we girls filled the water and feed containers and the boys removed the cow pies. Together we all climbed the stairs to drop down wedges of hay and straw bales down through the trap doors.

The loft was designed with trap doors over the mangers below, as well as one trap door in the middle of the loft. The middle door allows hay or straw to be dropped in the aisle to be spread on the floor of the chicks, turkeys and laying hens; or you open the trap doors along the edge of the barn and drop the hay into the mangers. Only Jeff, Alan and I walked to the front of the barn for hay bales. Gwenie went to the straw bales. She climbed the stack and sitting on the top, she pushed three bales off the edge with her feet. She climbed down and hooking her fingers into the twine around the bale, she pulled it toward the center of the loft. She slipped on the loft floor and fell backward on her bottom. She was so close to the open trap door that opened to the cement walkway nine feet (two hundred seventy five centimetres) below.

"Gwenie, what are you doing?" I screamed. "You want to fall out of the loft? What are you doing with a full bale? We cut the twine and carry wedges. What are you thinking?"

"Take a deep breath Jackie, Gwenie is okay." Jeff said. "You girls go put the hay and straw in with the chicks and turkey's pen and we will be right down, okay?"

"I wasn't close to the hole and I was just pulling the bale closer. I was not lifting it." Gwenie said indignantly.

I turned the water on, into the grate to flush the waste to the pit. Gwenie shook out the hay and straw into the bird's pen, in total silence.

"Shall we all take one red and one blue mineral block to the sheep pen, and then we can go lock the pigs in?" Jeff asked.

"Sure, that's a plan." I said after a minute of silence.

Jeff and I together lifted one red mineral salt block after lifting one blue one putting it in the little red wagon. Rules! Carrying anything weighing more than ten pounds (four and one half kilograms) was not allowed. If you couldn't share the lifting and transport it by wheels or sleigh, it was to be left undone and reported. Safety first and there is no exceptions. That is the Rules!

The sheep were so excited to see something new; they tried to crowd in close.

"I wish they would help us pull the wagon" Alan said as we made our way to the salt block house. "They sure like this. They eat a lot and it is not the weather that steals it with them covered by the enclosure. Dad thought they might last longer by keeping the blocks out of the weather, but I don't think so. I think it just motivates them to eat more at shoulder height."

"Yea, I heard him say that to Mom." I said. We walked together to the pig barn. All the purebred Yorkshire pigs had finished eating and were back in the barn. We closed Mr. Smith's pen gate. Mr. Smith is a purebred Yorkshire boar that is thirteen months old and weights seven hundred pounds (three hundred and eighteen kilograms). He loves to be scratched behind his ears. We locked the six Moms in and headed for the grain for our calves.

"Look at them running to the gate. You think they haven't been combed or fed in a month. They act like poor neglected babies." I said laughing as Jeff turned off the valves to the mash tank. Alan and Gwenie measured out four containers of grain.

Everyone was laughing at the calves crowding the gate as we carried the grain and comb to them. Ten minutes of brushing was just a start to what our 4-H calves wanted. You have to be nine years old to be in 4-H and have calves, but Gwenie and Alan have their calves and have done everything but become registered in the program. It is a perfect opportunity to get practice. The calves liked being petted and combed. After ten minutes, they tried to follow us out the gate, begging to be combed some more.

I filled a gallon bucket with grain for the horses. Lucy, Mom's horse, watched us so she unfastened the gate and headed to the stalls, in the barn, with the other six horses and George, the donkey, in tow. Unless the pasture gate is triple-locked, Lucy opens it whenever she wants and she and the others roam the farm with freedom from fences. When I arrived with the grain mixture, all seven horses, and George, were impatiently waiting in their stalls for their treat. They were listening to Mom singing from the milking parlour. Mom and Dad were washing the milking machines. Lucy decided it was more important for them to get their treat in the barn, instead of in the pasture, so she took it upon herself to lead the others into the barn for their morning and evening treats. Dad had joked about who was the boss of the ranch when Lucy first started this ritual. Mom said she wished Lucy would pay the bills too if she wanted to make decisions. They triple-locked the gate and took the grain to the pasture. Yet, as soon as the gate was unlocked, Lucy headed for the barn with the others, regardless of the fact that the grain was being delivered to the pasture.

"Hello!" Alan called as he was the first one in the barn after the horses.

"Hello!" called Mom and Dad, together. "We are finished our chores. The sheep need more hay tomorrow." said Jeff.

"Thank you. You know we just love our hard working little cowboys and cowgirls." said Dad. "Now, if you will close the gate after Lucy leads the herd back, you can go to the house and get ready for supper. We will be ten minutes behind you."

"Do you want to make biscuits tonight or do you want fresh bread?" asked Mom.

"Fresh bread," we all very loudly answered together.

"Still warm from the oven, yum," said Alan.

"Okay, off you go and we will be there soon, said Dad. "Love you," said Mom and Dad together.

"Love you too," we all answered together,

"I will lock Lucy up if you want to just go to the house," I said.

"Yes bossy," Jeff answered making us all laugh.

"Do you have homework, Gwenie?" Alan asked.

"Yes, I am so glad tomorrow is Friday. It has been a long week."

"Right," Jeff and Alan answered together and grinned.

"I have to read my Dick and Jane book," said Alan.

"Ugh," said Jeff . "I just have some math to do."

"I never checked the wood box, but let's each carry in an armful of firewood. One less trip if we need more," said Gwenie.

"Yea, one more armful each will fill it, adding Jackie's armful, said Alan, turning toward me coming in the door.

"You are really loaded with firewood. Are you under our weight restrictions?" Alan asked as I walked into the mud room loaded with firewood.

"Of course I am. I don't want any trouble," I said, as my sibling walked out for one more armful each.

"The house smells so great; it is making my mouth water. We will be able to change out of our barn clothes and set the table before Mom and Dad comes in." said Jeff , "not enough time for showers.

2

Go To School?

Gwenie was closest to the phone when it started ringing.

"Hello." Gwenie said. "Fine thank you Mr. McIntosh. How are you?... No, Mr. McIntosh, another five minutes anyway... I will have him call you as soon as he comes in.... Goodbye." said Gwenie.

"We haven't talked to Mr. McIntosh for two weeks and we sure get to talk to him a whole bunch today." said Jeff.

"Let's put little bread plates on the table tonight. I don't know if we are having stew so we need bowls or roast beef and vegetables so we need plates," said Alan. "And it will spoil the surprise if I peek."

"Mom and Dad are coming in now so we will not be kept in the dark for long. Hello." I said.

"Dad, Mr. McIntosh called and he would like you to call him as soon as possible." said Gwenie.

"Okay, I will slip into the office and give him a quick call. It will have to be a quick call with the best warm fresh bread in the world is waiting." said Dad.

"Yes! Hurry." we all called together, laughing.

"We have brisket with vegetables! That is my favourite." I said.

"Yippy," said Jeff, Gwenie and Alan.

"I'll get the buttermilk," I said, opening the fridge.

"I'll get the pickles. We sure do not need ketchup or mustard," said Jeff.

"I've got the bread plates on the table, and lots of butter," said Alan.

"Okay. Dad can come any time now," said Gwenie.

"You can each take a slice of bread and butter it. It will keep perfectly on your bread plates until Dad comes and says prayer." said Mom.

"I'm here. Please bow your heads. *Thank you Heavenly Father for all our Blessings. Thank you for this beautiful day. Bless us and all our friends, family, loved ones and neighbours. Guide us to do your will. Bless this beautiful feast to our bodies use in Jesus name we ask. Amen."* prayed Dad.

"Hey Kids. Do you want to go to school tomorrow?" asked Dad

"No!" we shouted.

"Is that your inside voice?" Mom said laughing with Dad joining in.

"Do you want to stay home and work really, really hard tomorrow?" Dad asked.

"Yes," we answered all at the same time.

"Okay we have a little problem to help with tomorrow. Can I wait till after supper to tell you so I can enjoy this beautiful supper hot?" asked Dad. "After all the problem will not go away."

"Okay," came out of each of our four mouths.

"Slow down your eating. You will not find out tomorrow's plan until Dad is finished and he is not in a rush," Mom said laughing.

"Mom, have you ever had such a quiet supper?" asked Dad.

"I think they thought if they stayed quiet we could eat faster." said Mom laughing, who was joined by us all at the table. Alan made a face to keep us laughing.

"Are you ready for dessert?" Mom asked. "No thank you." We all answered really fast that had everyone laughing again.

"Okay we will clean the table and have dessert after I tell you about tomorrow, okay? Dad asked.

"Yes, Please!" we shouted excitedly.

Dad told us that Mr. McIntosh has made arrangements for us 4-H in this area to help with the Kopple farm. Mrs. Jenkins knows we will not be on the bus. Gwenie and Alan are not registered 4-H but are included in the work bee. Now, when we finish chores here, in the morning, Dad will drive over and check on

Grandma Linda's farm and chickens. He will go pick Mr. Kopple up and take him to his Doctors at nine o'clock. Mom will make up a plate of our supper for Mr. Kopple and he needs dog food, tonight. Mrs. Kopple's Mother had some kind of accident so she took the three kids and went to her parents place about three weeks ago. Now the cows were not fed for a couple of days and the bull with the cows pushed on the fence stretching the wires trying to eat on the other side. Mr. McIntosh has fed them hay. We will take the little tractor over pulling the trailer with the wheelbarrow and pitch forks, rakes, and scoop shovels. Dad or Mom will mark them so we will know they are ours. We need tractors with buckets to clean the barns and farm yard. Scary is what Mr. McIntosh says that house is, quote, *'stinky rotten'*. Mrs. McIntosh knows of a product that will take the smoke smell of years away by washing down everything with it. Mrs. McIntosh has figured out to use car window washer squeegee things on poles to wash the ceilings and walls. That eliminates climbing ladders. A steam cleaner will be used for all fabric on the furniture and any carpet. They figure it will be no problem to have the whole house done in four hours if there are at least twelve folks working. All clothes, curtains, bedding, etc. needs washing, I am told. Kopples moved in with young twins, followed by a new baby and another one on the way so there has been no time for such deep cleaning. Everything will be washed in the house and the barns will be cleaned, as well as the paddock and the chicken coup. If the buildings and corral get cleaned in time, there are some repairs needed with fencing and apparently, the front porch has a couple of rotten boards we could change to make their home safe for them. The bull broke into the paddock where the milk cow was kept and she is fine as at least three calves are sucking her. Our Great Grandfather and crew built that beautiful elegant home before Dad was born. Mr. Kopple will have the dog locked in the outside enclosure, as he is not friendly to strangers. After a good sleep tonight we will help the neighbour tomorrow.

"Wow! I sure am glad Mr. McIntosh stopped to help us rescue that calf. We could be saving a real disaster." said Jeff .

"It will be so nice for Mrs. Kopple to come home with family to sweet smelling house. We will wear our work clothes tomorrow, and girls, we will wear scarfs on our heads so our hair won't get covered with splashes of cleaning product." said Mom.

"What is our job?" I asked.

"We will all find out tomorrow when Mrs. McIntosh gives us our choice of jobs." answered Mom. "Okay, dishes in the dishwasher and off to showers, you hard working farmers. Dessert will be served when Dad gets home."

"Wow! Exciting!" said Alan as we four climbed the stairs to our bedrooms.

"Can I shower first Jeff?" Alan asked.

"Sure, I can do my math while you shower first." Jeff said.

"Can I shower first Jackie?" Gwenie asked.

"Sure, I will go to Mom and Dad's bathroom." I said.

"I don't think you better, Jackie. Mom has not sat down for a minute all day with all the bread making and baking she did so I think she might come up for a soak in her tub after she gets the loaves of bread dealt with. Dad will not be home for at least forty-five minutes." said Jeff.

"Yes, you are probably right. I will do my homework while you shower first, Gwenie," I said.

3

THE HOUSE

Our home is the most beautiful. It is so open we can always see what is going on. There are eight wide steps that take us up to the huge deck where the barbecue and rocking chairs sit. The door opens to the mud room. There are eighteen hooks hanging on the wall for coats, plus a clothes closet to hang visitor coats. There are hat racks above the hooks and double layered boot rack below. Snow boots and barn boots are kept on the bottom rack. Next to the closet are lockers to keep our barn clothes. Two sinks in a long cabinet are on one wall, beside the door that goes into the bathroom. The washer and dryer for barn clothes are on the other wall beside a dresser. It holds our hats, gloves, scarves, mitts, glasses and flashlights. The wood box and wood burning stove are close to the very wide arch going into the kitchen.

The walk in pantry is beside the refrigerator. The cabinets wrap around two walls. The counter top ends with cabinet holding double ovens, with a pullout under the ovens for crockpots. Our island of cabinets in the middle is really wide and holds six stools. Our dining room table holds twelve chairs and the table behind it can hold the same when extended. The two walls of windows shine on the kitchen, dining room and family room, which is one huge room. There is a beautiful cabinet holding our stereo which plays the radio or our record collection. It is surrounded with couches and chairs, leaving us floor room to dance. A beautiful staircase rises up to the bedrooms. Behind it is the staircase to the basement. Behind the staircase on this floor is an office, bathroom and bedroom.

Upstairs, we have the best bedrooms. Gwenie and I each have a bedroom painted a soft pinkish colour with a white dresser, desk, chair and bunkbeds. We have a door beside our closet that goes into a bathroom, we share. The boy's rooms are painted a soft green colour with stained wood furniture and shared bathroom. Mom and Dad's bedroom is larger with a bathroom that has a bathtub plus a big shower and two sinks. Great Grandfather asked them if they were royalty. The last room upstairs holds a washer and dryer, linen closet and cabinet. Its octagon window opens to allow hanging clothes on a clothes-line.

Mom and Dad spent their honeymoon in this house. They said it was the most beautiful place in the world so why go anywhere else. I would like to design a home and be so proud of it I would spend my honeymoon in it.

Going down the stairs all the way to the basement opens into a huge recreation area; game tables, homework area, television, recliner chairs and patio doors to the yard. Our beautiful new recliner chairs was our only Christmas gift. A semi-truck with a load of recliners got into an accident. Mom and Dad were friends of the owner of the trucking company they knew from college. They purchased the whole truck load. We have six and our extended families and some close friends purchased the rest. There is an area set aside for sewing machines, with storage for sewing supplies and art projects. Next to it is the utility room. A bathroom and two bedrooms with shared bathroom complete the basement.

Under the deck is another play area. We have a small tepee and large sand box and toy box, holding all the toys we play with when younger company comes. A big barn with all kinds of animals is stored in the box. Tinker toy sticks to make corrals and fences are there with Lego blocks for making buildings.

We love helping our young cousins make farm yards in the sand box.

Great Grandpa built this house before he married. It was much smaller with no running water, no electricity, no natural gas and an outdoor toilet. A wood stove was used to cook, heat the house and heat the water that was carried into the house after you pumped it by hand out of the well. Grandpa Lorne was young when he helped build their new house on the land where they have their lumber yard. Great Grandpa and Great Grandma still live happily in that home.

Grandpa Lorne purchased this farm before he married Grandma Ella. They did different renovations over the years, putting in electricity, running water, gas and indoor plumbing. Dad grew up in this home.

Mom and Dad purchased this farm after college.. McCarthy's Lumber and Construction Limited built Grandpa Lorne and Grandma Ella's new home on the quarter of land east of here. When they finished that home they came here and started by lifting the whole house to put a new larger basement under it. Dad said he was tired of growing up with one bathroom for all the family. Mom and Dad designed an absolutely state-of-the-art home so Great Grandpa said. I just love this house as do my brothers and sister. We have the best home.

"Dad's home," called Jeff.

"Mom?" I called.

"I will be right down," Mom called from behind her closed bedroom door.

"Hello Dad," everyone said as Dad walked into the kitchen.

"Hello," Dad said as he walked to the bread box and pulled out a tray of berry strudel.

"Oh yea!" Alan cried, having every eye turned to the tray.

"Super!" said Jeff and Gwenie and I together, who made everyone, laugh, as Jeff handed me the glasses to fill with buttermilk. Dad put the tray on the counter and bounced up the stairs. Gwenie and Alan got the cutlery and napkins.

"We will starve if they don't hurry," Alan said making everyone laugh.

"What is so funny? Dad asked.

"We were worrying about starvation waiting for you," Alan said, laughing, which caused another outburst of laughter.

Dad sat down at the table and waited for Mom to join us before he said prayer.

All of us were in our pajamas except Dad.

"How is Mr. Kopple doing?" Mom asked.

"Not good, not good at all. He insists he will not go to hospital tonight but I will be there in morning. He says his dog barks at the dresser a couple times in the middle of the night, waking him up. The dog will not leave his bedroom at night, which is strange as he has never left the porch before. He said the dog is good company with his family gone." said Dad.

"The poor dog probably misses the babies' too." said Mom.

"Okay, my little cowboys and cowgirls. After you put your dishes in the dishwasher, please enter your hours in the time book and off to bed. It has been a long day with school, stopping to help the calf, chores, supper and now dessert. Please brush your teeth and say your prayers and we will be up to tuck you in before lights out. We will have you out of bed by six thirty tomorrow morning. We will do chores and after we finish breakfast, someone will have to drive the tractor over by nine o'clock." Dad said.

"Mom, you can drive and if we put the topper on we won't drown in dust when we ride in the back please?" said Jeff.

"If you are really sure, we can do that." Dad said.

"Yes!" came from our four mouths as we bounded up the stairs.

"We will be up shortly. Love you," said Mom.

"Love you too," we all called.

4

THE RIDE

"Is everyone up? Jeff called, as he turned off the alarm, hearing three more alarms ringing.

Jeff was the first one to get to the mud room. "Good morning, big day today." Alan said as he entered the mud room. Gwenie and I were right behind him. Jeff was putting on his coat.

"Everyone got a flashlight?" Jeff asked as he held the top drawer of the dresser open. With a nod from us three, he closed the drawer and we headed to chores.

Jeff opened the door and everyone filed out into the dark morning, without a word. Like robots, we silently worked together to get all the chores done. Entering the mud room together, we took off our boots, coats, hats, scarfs and gloves before we put the flashlights back in the drawer.

"Does anyone want hot oatmeal this morning," asked Jeff as we were all washing at the sinks.

"Yes please, I always get cold when it is dark out," said Gwenie.

"Sure," answered Alan and I, as I went to get the big pot out of the cupboard. I added salt and measured out three cups of water, before putting it on the burner.

Jeff pulled the buttermilk out of the fridge as well as our homemade saskatoon jelly and the strawberry jam.

Alan put six slices of bread in the toaster oven as Gwenie took the butter from under its glass container and slid it across the counter to Alan. She had to stretch to reach six glasses out of the cupboard, putting them on the counter within Jeff's reach.

Alan put the toast plates, bowls and cutlery on the counter.

"I am going to make another pot of coffee. There is not two cups left and I think it is a day that Mom and Dad need fresh coffee before we start on our adventure." said Gwenie. "I am surprised we didn't see Mom and Dad at all while we were doing chores."

"They finished milking, so they must be in the cream room. Oh, here they come with the tractor and trailer. Perfect timing," I said.

"Good morning," Mom and Dad said together as they entered the kitchen through the large arch, all washed up.

"Good morning," we all called at the same time.

"Breakfast is now being served," said Jeff with a big smile, and a bow as his arm directed them into the stools at the counter.

"Thank you my funny cowboy," Dad said as everyone laughed and sat on their stools. *"Heavenly Father, thank you for this beautiful day and the privilege you bestowed on us to help our fellow neighbour. Bless our families, friends, loved ones, neighbours and bless all whom are walking in your footsteps and asking for your help. Lord, bless us that we might be an honour to you as we work with our neighbours to help. Lord, Bless this food to our bodies use. We ask this in Jesus's name. Amen."* Dad prayed.

"Breakfast is delicious. We are so glad we taught you little angels to cook." said Dad.

"We are more proud to be your kids. No one can measure up to you. We learn to do everything and spend so much time riding and loving life. It is the Best." I said.

"Absolutely!" said Jeff, Gwenie and Alan together. "Our morning Bible lesson is so very appropriate," said Mom.

"It is Matthew7:12, Therefore, whatever you want men to do to you, do also to them. For this is the Law and the Prophets. What is this Bible text telling us?"

"That is our golden rule," I said, "Do unto others as you would like others to do onto you."

"Well, we know today's Bible lesson so we must get ready to leave now. I have to go pick up Mr. Kopple or we will be late for his appointment. It will take longer for you to get there by tractor, as well." said Dad.

"Yes, I love you," I said, echoed by Jeff, Gwenie and Alan.

"I love you more," said Dad, "and I will be with you shortly to help do my share."

"I love you little angels," said Mom, after Dad released her from hugs and kisses, and he messed our hair up on his way to his toothbrush. "Now we have all the dishes in the dishwasher, please brush your teeth and get your coats, hats and gloves on and we will be off shortly."

"I love you, Mom," said all us four as we crowded around Mom for a hug.

The sun was just peeking above the horizon, blessing us with the morning light. The sky to the east was dressed in shades of blue, pink and gold. Some clouds were picking up the combination of colours, stretching them as far as you could see. The top of the mountains were bathed in a crown of shining different shades of white. Diminishing layers of snow were running down the edges, showing off the crevices and valleys. Some rocks poked through giving us the promise of spring with the sun shining on them. The air smelled so fresh with a very light wind blowing from the west.

The trailer was hooked onto the tractor bar by a pinto hitch. The bar extends behind the tractor so whatever equipment is attached, it does not hit the tractor tires. A pinto hitch is a thick round metal circle, about six inches, (fifteen centimetres) in diameter. It is mounted on a metal plate that bolts to a machine. The one on the tractor bar is diagonal with the top half hinged to lift up.

It is designed to lock when it is closed. The trailer was the first truck Dad owned. When it was totally worn out, he removed the front axle, mechanical parts and cab off the frame. Uncle Bryan and Dad bent the frame so both sides came together three feet in front of the truck box. With the welder, they designed the hitch with the back of the pinto hitch bolted on it. This part of the pinto hitch is a thick round metal circle that lays horizontal. It drops into the diagonal ring and it is locked in. On the box is a camper top that is only two feet high. It has sliding windows all the way around it. Inside the trailer are all the pitchforks, shovels, rakes and our wheelbarrow. There are four little old milk stools also. We all crawled into the truck box and got comfortable on the stools with our heads inches from the roof.

"Okay, there are seven vents in this trailer topper that can be opened from the inside. You will want to adjust vents so you can get clean air and not dust from tractor tires. Every turn will probably mean different vents open with the little wind we have. Is everyone comfortable?" Mom asked.

"Yes," we answered.
Mom closed the end gate and topper back door, before she headed to the tractor.

"Oh, that vent doesn't work. We just got dust from it. This one works perfect." said Jeff.

"Corner, dust, dust, this one works without dust," said Alan. "Mom is stopping. She is walking back here."

"Is everyone doing well?" Mom asked. "Not too much dust?"

"We are perfectly fine, Thank you," we all called, as Mom closed the back door again.

The ruts and holes in the road are so rough. The old truck has no shocks on it. Every little rut makes the trailer jump so we have to hang on to the box to keep our stools under us. We thought the school bus was rough. It is like a ride in a Cadillac, compared to this. One bonus is we are travelling so very slow, we can really enjoy the countryside.

You can see fresh dirt on top of a mound. A gopher must have been out checking out the world to see if winter is over. Or maybe it was a hungry coyote digging to find a meal. It won't be long before we are on the land planting the crop for another year.

"Mom is stopping again. What's up? We will never get there." said Gwenie.

"We are all perfectly fine in here, Mom. Thanks for stopping but we are fine." said Jeff.

"Okay," Mom called as she got back on the tractor and got it moving again.

"This is too much. We don't have much more than a half mile (one kilometer) to go and Mom is stopping again. We are never going to get there on time at this rate." said Jeff.

"We're fine Mom; just don't want to be late." I called when I could see Mom out the topper window.

"That was three times she stopped to check on us. Do you want to play dead when we arrive?" said Alan.

"Yea, that should bring a laugh," said Gwenie.

"I hope so," said Jeff.

"She will be miffed but when everyone laughs, I guess it will be okay," I said.

"Okay, this is show time, Mom's stopping," said Jeff. Mom opened the topper door and truck box end gate. "Okay, we are here." There was a long period of silence. "Jacqueline Katherine, Jeffrey James, Gwendolyn Arleen, Alan Lorne, enough of this foolishness, now! Get up. You are not funny," Mom said as she stood at the back of the trailer, hanging onto the door.

"Surprise," I said and we opened our eyes to   see Mother with a red face. We all crawled to the back door.

No one was laughing. You could hear a pin drop as Mom walked toward the house.

"Mom,   we   are   sorry,"   Alan   called.

Mom   stopped.   "Apology   accepted.   Do   you remember what your Bible lesson was this morning?" Mom said as she turned and started walking toward the house again where Mrs. McIntosh stood.

We walked to the house very embarrassed.

No one was laughing. Not a word was said.

The house was huge and so elegant. In a heartbeat you could see what it was when it was new. Many stories were told of the parties from this home and the important people that attended. Now, the siding was dull and dirty. The front porch railings needed pant. The bushes in front needed cutting and shaped. The house looked tired but still elegant.

"Good morning to you all and thank you for coming," said Mrs. McIntosh. "If I can get some tall gentlemen, please, I will get you to reach all the drapes and curtains in the house, and bring them out, as well as the couch and chairs, and any lose carpets. Someone please check the basement. The rest of us can bring out all clothing, bedding, towels. Also, would you please move dressers and furniture into the center of the room so the walls can be washed easily and my helpers can wash furniture. Thank you gentlemen for your help for maybe ten minutes before Mr. McIntosh takes you away to the barn yard. We do not want a piece of cloth left in the house, Thank you." The inside of the house, if you could get past the smell of fat old cigar smell, was breathtaking. Walking in the front door brought you into a foyer that was open to a parlour on one side and a living room on the other. A beautiful winding staircase in carved wood extending to the second floor stood in the middle of the room. Behind it was a carved wood bar with shelves of glasses. The ceiling felt so high. Before reaching the dining room, there was a door leading into a library. Ceiling to floor books in carved wood bookcases that stretched across the entire wall. Leather chairs with carved wood legs and wood crown looked like something from a royal castle. The table in the dining room which has twenty chairs seated around it has huge carved legs. A very long china cabinet sits against the wall, which matches the table with all the same wood carving. Through the door brings you into a huge kitchen with lots of counter space and huge appliances. A large island was pushed to one wall so a small table with four chairs and three high chairs sat in the middle of the kitchen. A pantry, the size of a small bedroom was off the kitchen. Next was a staircase to the basement, a bathroom and laundry room, and a door leading out to the back yard deck. Going up the stairs, found a huge foyer with easy chairs. Five bedrooms completed the upstairs with two of the bedrooms having their own bathroom. The house was now stripped of all fabric and the men and boys headed to the barnyard.

"Jacqueline and Gwendolyn, do you want to work together?" asked Mrs. McIntosh.

"Yes, we can, Mrs. McIntosh," I answered as Gwenie nodded her head.

"Okay, that is great girls. I am going to wash the ceiling and walls in the babies' room. If you two will grab a pink pail, and those cloths, I need you to wash every square inch of the furniture, bed, and mattress, everything I cannot get with the squeegee." said Mrs. McIntosh.

"That did not take too long. You girls are great. You can move into the master bedroom as I finish here." said Mrs. McIntosh.

"Lets do the mattress, and the bed first so we can put the washed drawers on it, okay?" I asked Gwenie.

"Yes, I sure don't feel like talking. I have never seen Mom so red with embarrassment. I feel terrible," said Gwenie.

"Me too," I said.

A blood-curdling scream erupted from our mouths in the master bedroom before we two girls clambered out the door and down the stairs, nearly knocking Dad off his feet as he was coming up.

"Spider! Spider!" Gwenie screamed as she trembled in Dad's arms, with me crowded in among them.

"Big, big spider, as big as my palm and dirty brown." I said in a less deafening tone.

Dad turned us girls around and headed us up the stairs followed by everyone that was down stairs, and everyone peering into the bedroom, from upstairs. This spider has the Kopples in a bad way with bad bites on him so they have put him in the hospital. The search is on to find the culprit, so they know what to treat him with. Dad entered the bedroom searching for the spider We all stood in the hallway watching through the open door.

Girls, where was the spider?" Dad asked.

"We turned the mattress to wash the edges and he was on the edge," I said.

"Dad, the elephant is moving!" Gwenie screamed.

"Honey, if that ceramic elephant starts marching around the top of this dresser, we are all in big trouble," Dad said laughing, followed by all fourteen ladies and girls laughing.

The ceramic elephant stood about eighteen inches, (forty six centimetres) high. It was sitting on the dresser. Its trunk was up over its head. It was about thirty inches, (seventy six centimetres) long. It had to be from Mexico or a South American country. It was hand painted with all kinds of bold colours. It is a real treasure to brighten up any room.

"Okay, will someone go get me some duct tape please. Good eyes Gwendolyn. This spider has a hole in between the front elephant legs so I think it is inside," Dad said.

The elephant was taped up and taken out to the middle of the driveway. If it tried to escape, there was room to catch it by putting the glass jar over it, which one of the ladies brought out. The elephant was laid on its side to show the duct tape. Minutes felt like hours as we watched the elephant to make sure the spider did not escape. Finally Dad came out of the house, waking to where we were standing guard. Dad told us it was all safe for us to go back to work. I am going to take your friend, the spider to the hospital. We stood there with our mouth open, thinking what to say about being accused of having that dangerous ugly spider for our friend. Dad blew the truck horn. Getting Mr. McIntosh's attention, he yelled to him for all to come for coffee break. He was laughing when he waved goodbye to us, as he was driving to town. We shook off the shivers, as we walked toward the house.

"Quon's grocery donated apples and some containers of pastries, when he found out what was going on here.

Mr. McCarthy brought them back with him when he was on the spider capture," said Mrs. McIntosh. "We have tea, coffee or soda pop to go with it."

"Thank you, just an orange crush will do me," I said.

"Grape crush for me, thank you," said Gwenie.

Everyone took what they wanted and sat around the front porch and on the wide stairs leading up to the porch. After fifteen minutes, Mrs. McIntosh let everyone know the bus would come and take us to lunch so we had better get back to work if we wanted to finish.

Work in the master bedroom was done with caution as we searched for more spiders. Mrs. McIntosh was also happy to finish the work without running into another spider. Going down the clean staircase, we found Jennifer and Janice coming out of the parlour. We can all start on the library. The upstairs is finished and three major rooms are finished down stairs, so that leaves us with the library. All the books must be washed. To do the pages, hold the book closed really tightly and with just a damp cloth, wash the page edges, then wash the front, back and spine of the books. The shelves must all be washed thoroughly before we put the books back in, we were told. We were all happy to start on the last room.

"Are you two okay?" asked Jennifer who is my age and in my class at school.

"No, we just feel sick," I said. "We thought we would be funny but it wasn't and it embarrassed Mom in front of you all and she is the best Mother in the world. I have so misbehaved, and me at my age, to not stop the foolishness, I could just die, for embar-rassing her and us."

"Love always makes it blow over, I promise. I have done some stupid things and it really does blow over," said Jennifer.

"Thanks," I said and the work overtook all conversation. Books, book shelves, chairs, windows, walls, and ceilings were all being washed as more ladies and girls were finished their areas and joined the cleaning of this last room. With so many hands, it was not long before the cleaning was finished and the floor was washed behind us as we left the room. Walking out the front door, with our buckets and cloths, we found new planks nailed on the front porch. We all went to the garden hose and washed out our buckets and rinsed our cloths. We dumped the cloths into the one large pail, and enjoyed a cold drink from the hose. The steam cleaner was cleaned and sat beside the large pail. All the upholstered furniture and carpets covered the patio, basking in the sun drying.

That will end our cleaning work here, and if you look yonder, here comes the bus." said Mrs. McIntosh laughing. Two of the dads were driving tractors out to the drive-way from the pasture. The rest of the men and boys were walking behind them. One dad stopped and closed the gate. The pasture looked cleaned and it looked like there was a new ramp in the little door of the chicken coop. The wires on the fence were all tight and the animals looked content, milling around their hay bales. The bus swung around the circular driveway and stopped, facing the road. The bus door opened and we were all told to climb aboard. Lunch was being served at the church hall.

5

White with Blue Candles

"All aboard," called Mrs. Jenkins, "Next stop is lunch."

"We have four passengers to pick up at McCarthy's first," said Mrs. McIntosh.

Minutes later, the bus pulled into our driveway and circled around in front of our barn. A few more windows were slid open on the bus as Mr. McIntosh, Susie, Mom and Dad boarded the bus.

The adults talked a little among themselves, as the boys talked about the breeds of the cattle and which one looked like a champion ribbon winner. We girls giggled at the boys and talked about having a home as beautiful as Kopples. The bus pulled into the church parking lot in record time, and we all got off.

"Everyone washed?" called Mr. McIntosh, as he stood close to the table of food.

"Let us all bow are heads and say the Lord's Prayer."

"Our Father which art in heaven,

Hallowed be thy name. Thy kingdom come
Thy will be done in earth, as it is in heaven.
Give us this day our daily bread.
And forgive us our trespasses,
as we forgive those who trespass against us.
And lead us not into temptation,
but deliver us from evil.
For thine is the kingdom,
the power, and the glory,
forever and ever.
Amen."

"Hard working young ones fill your plates first," said Mr. McIntosh.

"Do the female folk have to share the male tables?" asked Butch to his father.

"I don't think it would be polite to have our hard working folks separated. Lunch is always better with company," said Butch's dad.

"But Dad, they smell like the places Sherlock Holmes describes in his books," said Butch.

"The room erupted in laughter.

"Son, it could be a lot worse, and they done a marvelous job getting the smoke out of that house and I promise you it was never an opium den as was stated in Sherlock's book." said Butch's dad.

A hum of chatter and laughter echoed in the hall.
"I cannot swallow a bite of this delicious hamburger," I said.

"I can't either," said Jeff , Gwenie and Alan. "Okay, it was my idea, so I am going to apologize publicly," said Alan.

Alan stood up and walked a short distance in front of the table. He was followed by Jeff, Gwenie and I.

"Mom, I am the one who came up with the idea to play dead. We have seven vents in that trailer we open from the inside and you stopped three times in the short trip to make sure we were okay, and I thought it was such over kill, you worrying about us, so much, we thought we would pull a funny prank. I am so sorry Mom," said Alan.

"Mom, I know better, and I am so sorry." I said.

"You done what?" yelled Dad laughing, causing everyone in the hall to join in in the laughter.

"Honey, I told you all, I accepted your apology," said Mom, who was laughing.

"Yea, but we don't feel better," We wanted it to be funny. We wanted everyone to laugh, not embarrass you," said Jeff .

Mom and Dad together walked to us, who were just standing there.

Dad, still laughing, with a bunch of the crowd, hugged us four kids.

As Mom was hugging us, she asked, "Can I turn this into a 4-H lesson?"

"Yes," we all replied, embarrassed.

"Pranks, we all like to pull pranks occasionally. Pranks are only good if no one gets hurt and it is funny. This prank did not come off funny. Now let us all 4-H members take a page from this note book. Now, a prank, here is an example, you all seen the dessert table as you walked by for your lunch. All those cookies and squares and that bag of marshmallows, I heard comments about. Now if I slipped over and covered the table with a matching table cloth, I can just imagine the faces I would see, looking at the table and seeing only table cloth until someone figured it out. Now that would be a real laugh. So let us tuck this trailer experience in our back pockets and have a great day. Everyone worked so hard. Thank you." said Mom as she walked us back to our table, and Dad hugged Mom on the way back to the adult table.

"Hello, my name is Susie, and I got something to say. Mom, can I sit on top this table so everyone can see and hear me?" Susie asked.

"Yes, do you need help, honey?" her Mom asked.

"I made it!" Susie said

"May I introduce my daughter Susie? She started talking before she could walk. I believe she will be the next Prime Minister of Canada," said Mr. McIntosh, making everyone laugh.

"How old are you Susie?" asked Mr. Thompson.

"I will be five in eight months," she replied to the laughter of all.

"I need to tell you all about Mrs. McCarthy. I was her special helper. We loaded up all the clothes, and sheets, blankets, drapes and curtains and put them in my Mom and Dad's truck and took them to her place. We slid the wringer washer, out the back door of the barn with three tubs and two stands as it was too nice to not be in the sunshine. She put my Mom's special product in the water and we rinsed everything in that water. We put them through the wringer. Then we would put them in a tub of cold clean water. We put them back through the wringer and put them in the laundry baskets. We even had to wash the laundry baskets in the water. Everything smelled fresher. Mrs. McCarthy put work clothes in the dirty tub water and we put three baskets full of rinsed clothes on a wagon and pulled it to the house. We took a load of sheets up the stairs and she put it in the washer with soap and some vinegar. We went to the mud room and put some blankets in that washer with soap and vinegar. She dumped a load of rinsed blankets on the floor so we could take the three empty baskets back to the barn with us, on the wagon. We changed water and done a whole bunch more loads, and then we started putting curtains in the water. They were a yucky yellow-brown but when they came out of the water, they were white with pink flowers and blue ribbons. They were just beautiful. We had to change the water after a few more pairs of curtains. Then, Mrs. McCarthy added some more product to the water. We shoved them ugly brownish drapes from the living room into the water and they came out gold. They were a real pretty gold colour with some brown stripes on them, still. We put them back in the water. We pulled the wagon with the three baskets to the house and Mrs. McCarthy took a laundry basket of more sheets and baby clothes up the stairs. Mrs. McCarthy opened the huge eight sided window with a funny closet beside it that opened to the window and not the room. She pulled out this clothes line. We hung those sheets on it and it just went out that window to dry among the tree tops. We put another load in and we went to the mud room and emptied that machine and filled it again and we went to the porch and hung up all those blankets. We got the beautiful gold drapes out of the water without any brown spots. We were rinsing them when my Dad and Mr. McCarthy drove into the barn with the tractor and a cow in the bucket. The cow was lying in the bucket with its leg hanging at a funny angle and it was making a funny noise. They slid this huge barn door open and then this hoist slid out on the roof with belts hanging down. The men put on these funny cover-over-alls and Mr. McCarthy nodded at us and Mrs. McCarthy took me to the house for buttermilk and to check the washing. I heard the gun fire before we got to the house. We had an excellent glass of buttermilk and a muffin. We went upstairs and hung up more clothes and put more in the washer. Did I tell you, that eight sided window will close to keep the weather out with the clothesline outside? We went back to the barn and rinsed some more clothes and washed and hung some more clothes. Then we did some clothes with grease on them. The product would not take all the grease out of them. Mrs. McCarthy went and got two bottles of coke-a-cola. I didn't want that stuff as the buttermilk was so good. She laughed and after we rinsed those greasy clothes, Mrs. McCarthy dumped the coke on the grease spots. She dumped them in the wringer washer and they washed. There were no grease spots when they came out of the washer. The tractor was backed out of the barn so I wondered up to the open door, when Mrs. McCarthy was hanging clothes on the clothesline at the barn. Mr. McCarthy was washing down that room that has meat saws, and hamburger making grinder, like we have that you have to turn by hand and all kinds of other machines and knives. It was all made of shiny metal so everything washed up quick and clean. Mr. McCarthy opened the cooler and showed me four pieces of the cow hanging up and the hide was wrapped up on the floor and a wheelbarrow full of innards that Mr. McCarthy said he will give to the pigs tonight. There was also a pan of heart, and liver and stuff and stuff to make sausages from, I think, and a big pail, I think it was blood. And the bus came, so as soon as Mr. McCarthy and my Dad took off their cover-over-alls and put them on the floor in front of where the washer usually sits, we all got in the bus. I want a farm just like theirs when I'm grown up. They are the nicest folks."

"Thank you Miss Susie. That was quite a speech. I recorded it for our first 4-H speech and you have

100%. You can use that when you are nine or by then you might have a better speech," said Mr. Holmes.

Everyone clapped and whistled as Susie returned to her burger, with a huge smile on her face.

"Mr. McCarthy do you have some news for us?" asked Mr. McIntosh.

"I think Miss Susie told you near everything. Mr. Kopple is in the hospital with spider bites. We managed to catch the spider, thanks to Gwendolyn's dancing ceramic elephant. Mrs. Kopple has one bite as well that they are treating at her Mom's town.

Mr. Kopple's parents were sent that elephant for Christmas, that did not arrive until a month ago, from South America. They knew Mrs. Kopple loved elephants so they gave it to her before she went to her Mothers. Mr. Kopple said the dog would sleep in his bedroom and bark at the dresser different times at night so maybe he was saved from more bites. He is really sick yet, but getting better by the minute now he has proper medication. The cow was caught in the north west fence and had busted her leg trying to get free. We could do nothing but try and preserve her meat. The deep freeze is pretty empty at the Kopples, so I don't think it will be too much of a hardship for them. I think Miss Susie covered near everything else except, we will have to look after their place for a week, anyway. I feel so thankful that I could be part of this helping the neighbour. Thank you!" Dad said.

"I would like to thank all the farm boys and men, for helping in the house and farm yard. I would like to thank all the girls and ladies who helped with the cleaning. I would like to thank the cooks who put this fantastic lunch on for us, as well as our bus driver Mrs. Jenkins. We could not have accomplished much without every one of your help. Thank you," said Mrs. McIntosh.

"It was my pleasure to be of some help. We have to leave here in twenty minutes so I can deliver you home and go pick up the kids who went to school," said Mrs. Jenkins.

Lorrel, who was sitting next to Jeff called out, "Mom, someone rented this hall so we have a wedding to set up for tomorrow. Can we do it now? All this help, it shouldn't take more than ten minutes."

"Excellent idea," said Lorrel's Mom. "We need twelve round tables, behind the dance floor, eight chairs per table. Two rectangle tables for the brides party of ten, in front. Two rectangle tables for gifts along that wall and two for their buffet, on this side please, close to the wall. Put the white table cloths with the blue doilies, and formal setting with wine glasses, please. Oh Thank you, I just wasn't thinking as far as tomorrow," said Mrs. McIntosh.

Everyone got into moving tables and adding chairs where they needed to be. White table cloths with blue crocheted doilies were added to the tables. A parade of dishes, glasses, cutlery and blue napkins were carried from the kitchen, which was hidden behind a wall at the end of the hall. Blue candles and wine glasses were added to the tables.

"Done, in twelve minutes," called Lorrel.

"Mom," called Susie, "do we need the little square table for the wedding cake?"

"Yes, please. Thank you, Susie. Boys, carry the table over beside the wedding party table and Susie, please come and I will get you the little table cloth and doily, and then let's race to the bus."

"The room looks beautiful with the blue doilies, napkins, and candles, and wine glasses. It sure would have taken us more than twelve minutes to do it. Thank you all. They are leaving the tables set up for us for Sunday lunch, after church. This is a crazy week. Thank you for all your excellent help," said Mrs. McIntosh.

"We are 4-H members. We help! It was a fun day," echoed loud, loud, and louder on the bus, making everyone laugh.

6

HOMEWARD BOUND

"All Aboard! Where is my first stop?" Mrs. Jenkins asked.

"Kopple's, please, our trucks are there," replied eight families.

"I have little bottles of product sitting on the front porch. Please take one and dump it into a half tub of water and rinse all the clothes you are wearing in it and then in cold water before you wash them and they will be fresh as new," said Mrs. McIntosh.

"Good Bye, Thank you" was shared by all as nearly all got off at the Kopple farm.

"Mom, can sis and I go home?" asked Lorrel.

"Yes you can and thank you," said Mrs. McIntosh.

"I can drop you off as soon as I go to McCarthy's farm, unless you want to catch a ride with one of the three families passing your gate." said Mrs. Jenkins.

"I need a shower, and my sister needs two showers so I know Butch's dad will drop us off. Okay Mom?" asked Lorrel.

"Yes, honey. You two enjoy your afternoon and we will be home as soon as possible. Thanks for all your help." said Mrs. McIntosh.

"Bye, thanks for all your help," was called from the bus as the two hurried to the truck Butch was just crawling into.

"Next stop is the McCarthy's," Mrs. Jenkins said.

"Such a productive day, I feel good," said Mr. McIntosh.

"U bet," said Dad, "We got more work done than I dreamed possible."

"Gentleman, will you each open a couple windows at the back of the bus before you get off. I think it will be aired out before I get to town. This bus and me does not smell like roses." said Mrs. Jenkins.

"Life is funny, we never know what surprises a day will bring" said Mom as we all got off and waved goodbye as the dads joked with Mrs. Jenkins, on their way off.

"Okay, we have the McIntosh's truck and tractor here and our truck and tractor with trailer is at Kopples." said Dad.

"If you dad's want to take the tractor, we will just do some laundry and we will be behind you so we can all check the house together and see how it smells now," said Mom. "Maybe carry the furniture back in, if it is dry.

"Sure," Dad said, "see you little angels shortly.

"Mom, you know we can do the laundry if you want to go and see what we have done today," I said. "Susie explained exactly how you rinsed the laundry."

"Are you sure? There is at least five more loads to wash and hang," Mom said.

"We got this, don't worry," said Jeff.

"Okay, see you soon. Love you!" said Mom, as the tractor was pulling out of the yard with both cowboys waving.

Mom and Mrs. McIntosh followed the tractor with Mrs. McIntosh driving her truck.

"Okay, girls, you know I am your respectful brother, but please do not go near the house. I am nearly sick of the smell of smoke on you. If you two will go shower in the barn, Alan and I will bring you clean clothes, hairbrushes, a crown if you like as you are princesses," said Jeff, making us all laugh.

"Yea, I am making myself sick. We are so lucky that none of our family smoke when it seems it is such a habit of so many families," said Gwenie. "I wonder what Great Grandfather would have said if he had come to the house today after building that house for those rich people, what, forty years ago?"

"Yea," Alan called over his shoulder as he and Jeff hurried to the house.

"Let's get clean clothes for us. I think we smell by association. We can shower in the barn after the girls so we don't stink up the place. Oh my boots smell. I am going to throw them out on the deck and we can get some of that solution that they are talking about and wipe down our boots and our belts. We might as well do all the boots with the saddle soap, once we have the smell off them. Let us check the lockers to see if everything we need is here so we do not have to run upstairs. It is crazy, I feel like I am a big cloud of bad smell that will vaporize in the house as a bad demon if I don't hurry." Jeff said, laughing.

"Me too. I have four paper bags we can put our clothes in," Alan said as he closed the cabinet.

"Good work," said Jeff, "I was just concentrating on getting out of the house fast."

"I got Gwenie's and mine," said Alan.

"Great, I got Jackie's and mine," said Jeff, "Let us take clean boots with us. We can rescue our boots from the deck and at least wear them to the barn.

"Hello," said Jeff.

"Hello," I called, "please leave my clothes at the door away from my stinky clothes and Gwenie is in the upstairs shower."

"Okay," said Jeff through the closed door, as he put the bag containing my clean clothes and boots down, close to the door. He put his clothes and boots beside mine and took the dirty clothes and boots walking toward the back of the barn. He met Alan coming down the stairs carrying Gwenie's stinky clothes and boots.

"I guess they couldn't stand the smell of their clothes in the shower room with them," Alan said, laughing. "This is just too funny. How did those neighbours live in their house smelling like that?"

"Beats me," Jeff said as he dropped the clothes into a tub that was half full of a kind of brownish colored water. "Let's use these old cloths and wipe down the boots with that water."

We are so proud of Great Grandfather. He told all his kids, grand kids, and great grand kids, if we have money to burn, we should do more charity work. He told everyone if we have to burn our money up in tobacco, we could not smoke or chew in any buildings. All the restaurants allowed you to smoke, inside. But, his word is law and I have not found a law from him that doesn't make perfect sense. Can you imagine the house smelling stale smoke all the time? Can you imagine us smelling like this? The Jorstad kids and Werner kids must have a hard life, the way they come to school smelling of smoke. Great Grandpa tells us that folks who don't smoke or smell smoke will live longer and be healthier.

"I'll get the saddle soap," said Jeff , sliding off the edge of the clothesline platform, in his sock feet, leaving Alan, and four pair of boots and belts sitting in the sunshine.

"The girls are finished," Jeff said as he laid the container of saddle soap, cloths and boot brushes on the platform.

"Great. You think we were cleaning out the sewage pit Oh give me the pigs over smoke, any day," Alan said laughing as we both walked sock foot to our showers.

"Gwenie, let's take these rinsed clothes to the house and check how many more loads of wash to do. Wow, the wagon is full,"

"U bet," said Gwenie, "Hey, I am just going to stay here on the deck and fold all these blankets from the line."

"Super, I am going upstairs to the laundry room," I said. The air was so fresh with a breeze that brushed the mountains on the way over the land. The sun slowly made its way across the sky.

"Wow, shiny mud room, Gwenie," said Jeff .

"Thanks, felt like cleaning, Jackie is upstairs. Hey would you two like to do the basement, or do you need down time?" asked Gwenie.

"I need work myself, my brain hurts to think," said Alan.

"Me too," said Jeff . "I just don't know how to fix the embarrassment we caused Mom."

The basement was looking pretty shiny when the boys heard Gwenie yell.

"Mom and Dad are home," yelled Gwenie.

Jeff and Alan raced up the stairs meeting me as I came down the stairs. We all skidded to a halt in the mud room when Mom and Dad walked in.

"Well hello," said Mom and Dad together.

"Wow! Stop! Out! We will bring you clean clothes to the barn. Gag, gag. Wow!" Jeff said as we all tried to hide our noses. "What have you been doing? Wow!"

Laughing, Mom and Dad stepped outside again, closed the door and headed to the barn.

"They have been gone over three hours and they come home smelling like that. I don't understand. I thought we had that house clean smelling. I wonder what is up. I don't think we smelled that bad did we?" I asked.

"I really don't think you girls smelled that bad. Hey, Alan, grab two bags, please. We will get them clean clothes and do their boots and belts, and start chores. Oops, our clothes are all still soaking, I will rinse them and bring them in to wash, after we rinse Mom and Dads." said Jeff.

"Hey, can you guys do chores for me tonight? I will make supper. How about macaroni tomato soup with meatballs and grilled cheese sandwiches? I asked.

"Sure, that will be no problem. Hey, we will do the calves after supper, okay?" asked Jeff.

"Thanks," I said turning toward the kitchen.

"Gwenie, if you take Mom's clothes and boots, and Jeff, if you will take Dad's clothes and boots I am going to open the doors on the truck. I think it might need it." said Alan. Jeff has Mom and Dad's belt and boots washed before Alan came pulling the wagon.

"What have you got there, Alan?" asked Jeff.

"I had to go get the wagon as I found a basket full of stinking drapes in the back of the truck and Mr. Kopple's clothes and boots in a bag in the front of one stinking truck," laughed Alan. "I do not know where they found these. They said the house was finished. This is strange."

"Okay, I will soak Mr. Kopple's clothes and we can do his belt and boots. I got Mom and Dad's done. Then we can do chores. Gwenie is already started with the chickens." said Jeff.

"Hello Jackie," called Gwenie from the mud room.

"We are finished chores. Alan and Jeff are rinsing Mom and Dad's clothes and will be in. Do you need anything from the cream room before I take off my boots?"

"Yes, please. A gallon of buttermilk, a pound of butter, and two dozen eggs please." I answered.

7

ROUGH TONGUE

"Hello," said Mom and Dad as they walked through the arch to the kitchen.

"Hello, we answered all at the same time as we went to them for hugs.

"Oh Dear," said Mom, "Comfort food and four heavy hearts. Dad we need your help."

"I have never seen four little angels work so hard and get so much done in one day with such heavy hearts. Let us fix that now."

"Heavenly Father, we thank you for this beautiful day and the privilege of working with our neighbours to help one of ours. Thank you for Blessings you have bestowed on us. Thank you for our daily bread. Heavenly Father, please use my wife and I and put your words in our mouth to help my children understand your unconditional love and forgiving nature and to help them understand your Peace in their hearts. Bless us and our family, friends,

neighbours, and loved ones. We ask this is Jesus name. Amen." prayed Dad.

"Jacqueline, only tears of happiness are allowed at the table." said Dad.

"I'm trying," I said as more tears slid down my cheeks. My siblings joined in with tears falling down their cheeks.

"Matthew 7:7, Ask and it will be given to you: seek, and you will find: knock and it will be opened. Do you know what this means?" asked Dad.

"Yes," we all answered at once.

"Did you ask our Heavenly Father to forgive you for a prank that just did not turn out very funny?" asked Dad.

"Oh Yes!" we all said, answering truthfully together.

"Did our Heavenly Father forgive you? Did we forgive you? Your friends forgive you?" asked Dad.

"Yes," we answered.

"Who does that leave to forgive you?" Dad asked.

"Our selves," I said.

"Now if our Heavenly Father asks you to forgive one another with love to get peace in your heart, do you think it might extend to you forgiving yourself? If I knocked the buttermilk off the table, and spilt it all over the floor, you would immediately forgive me and help me clean up the mess. Now it is up to me to forgive myself for such a silly action that caused that. Being mad at myself is not going to pick up the buttermilk and put it back in its jug on the table. Being mad at myself will not help me to enjoy your company or my supper. When Heavenly Father wants me to forgive everyone else, do you think it might be even more important to forgive ourselves? Forgive, but not forget the lesson, so if we are ever tempted to try to make the same or similar mistake, you will laugh and say, oh no, I am not doing that again. I remember how that made me feel. Once of that foolishness was all I needed to learn that lesson for life. And, you know, we all seem to have to make our own mistakes so we can remember them and learn by them." said Dad.

"Oh Dad, I forgot we talked about this before. You are so right. I am going to forgive myself and remember this lesson. My heart doesn't hurt anymore. It hurt so badly all day." I said as I got off my chair for a real hug, with tears of relief falling.

"Thank you for your light hearted hugs," Mom said. "It hurts me worse to see you hurting than it hurts you."

"Oh I have been so ashamed of myself for embarrassing you. I have friends at school whose parents do not teach them to knit, crochet, sew, cook, garden, clean, skate, swim or anything. They are told to go watch television and stay out from under their feet. One of my friends never knows whether her parents will come home from the Beer Parlour. We are the luckiest kids in the whole world. I am so sorry." I said.

"Exactly right," said the other three.

Mom and Dad smiled at each other and then started to laugh. We joined in the laughter. We seem to always come up with the same words at the same time that is just too funny. We were all still laughing when we sat down again after our hugs.

"Please forgive yourself for one minute of a bad action, as it is erased from everyone who forgave you. Now, we have some news for you, if you have had enough hugs. Only half the news tonight Dad, will be enough," Mom said with a twinkle in her eye.

"What? What news?" we asked.

"Okay, Jacqueline, I understand you have made a feast of macaroni tomato soup with meatballs and grilled cheese sandwiches. Do you think this hard working family should eat before they hear more tales of a long day?" Dad asked, laughing.

"Oh, this is delicious. Thank you honey, I am so happy you still had the energy to feed us tonight." said Mom. What have you done since we left you at home?"

"Gwendolyn, you go first please," said Dad.

"I had a shower first. The boys went and got our clothes and we showered in the barn. I came to the house and I folded all the dry blankets off the line, on the deck. I hung up wet blankets and done a couple loads of clothes and hung them up to dry. I cleaned the bathroom in the mud room and I cleaned the mud room and some of the closets and drawers, and folded more dry clothes off the line. I did chores. That's all."

"Wow. And the mud room looks beautiful and I know it was done with hard work. Thank you." said Mom "That was a lot of work. Thank you," said Dad.

"Alan, what did you do?"

"I helped Jeff get all our clean clothes and boots. I showered. I helped rinse clothes and wash our boots and belts and saddle soap them. I helped fold all the dry clothes on the line at the barn, and hung up more clothes. I helped soak the coveralls in salt, or should I say cover-over-alls like Susie calls them. After we finished the clothes at the barn, we brought them here to the deck and then went to clean the basement. I found Mr. Kopple's boots and belt and clothes in your truck. I took them and got the wagon for all those drapes from the back of the truck and pulled them to the barn. I soaked Mr. Kopple's clothes and I washed Mr. Kopple's boots and belt, as Jeff finished your boots and belts. We soaked the drapes. We have done chores. Oh, I left the doors open in your truck to air out and I thought I might wash it out after we do our 4-H calves. That's all." Alan said.

"Wow, that is a lot and we haven't checked to see how the basement looks, but I know it is great." said Dad. "Thank you."

"Jeffrey?" asked Dad.

"Everything Alan said plus the last pair of drapes are soaking right now," said Jeff. "It was a beautiful afternoon to be out in the sunshine. "Our boots look so great; I am thinking we should do our saddles soon." "With all the work you done today, you are think of more work. We are so proud of you all," said Dad. "Jacqueline?" asked Dad.

"I had a shower and went upstairs. I folded clothes and hung out some wet ones and washed a load and hung it up too. I starched curtains. I made supper. That's all." I said.

"Wow, how many curtains did you starch?" asked Mom "I am on my very last pair of curtains," I said. "Wow, well we know how you all worked, like each of you doing the work of three people today. You are amazing. You will all write twelve hours in your allowance time books for today, plus twelve hours for tomorrow as you have been out of bed for over twelve hours already today. We just love you so much. We cannot believe how hard you all worked today and for so long." said Dad.

"We have the best kids in the world. I love you and I am so sorry you worked so hard today." said Mom.

"We love you," we said together, making us all laugh.

"Okay, let's clear the table for cookies and you can hear about our day," said Mom.

"Us four decided to check the house one last time when we arrived. When we walked into the library, a book did not look cleaned. I pushed on it and the wall slid in and moved sideways to open to a very smelly gentleman lounge which was worse than the whole house as it was closed off and sealed. The four of us washed every square inch of that room; steam cleaned the carpet and then went searching for more hidden rooms. We brought the dirty drapes home. We will all go over tomorrow and with the McIntoshes, we will put the house back together and Great Grandfather will meet us there too. He wants to see the house again." said Dad.

"I pulled on that book but it wouldn't come off the shelf so I washed it on the shelf but it would not polish up like the rest of the books," I said laughing. "Funny."

"Okay, No more work tonight. Go brush your calves and television or quiet time. Whatever you hard working angels want." said Mom with tears in her eyes.

Mom moved into Dads arms as we went through the arch to get our coats and boots on.

"Shall we play dead to our calves with their combs in our hands?" asked Alan laughing as we picked up our calf's combs.

"I think I played dead enough today," I said laughing.

"Can you believe Butch and the rest of them did not even tease me at all today, and they let me work alone?" said Jeff laughing.

"We were not so funny but now Dad has straightened us out, it is funny how silly we tried to be. I will think three times before I try and pull a prank again," said Gwenie.

"I worked so hard upstairs with the clothes and starching the curtains and I was trying to get the ironing board to just swallow me, into a perfect storybook world," I said.

"I looked in the mirror after my shower and I felt so guilty I wanted it to pull me through it into some fantasy land ," said Gwenie, "Alice in Wonderland."

"If Jeff had not insisted I work with him, I thought of walking West down the road and forget to stop walking, but then I knew it was all my idea and I didn't want to leave you all with all the shame. We know we are loved and forgiven but it is still hard to accept our foolishness," said Alan.

"Just one minute of stupid thinking, by us all, that we all acted on, cause us to have such a guilt ridden, ashamed of ourselves day. What is worse, it effected everyone because we didn't work together, laughing and kidding each other like our work bees are always like," said Jeff.

"They even felt bad for us when we apologized at lunch. They knew we couldn't swallow lunch," I said.

"After lunch, Susie said, she was sure glad it was us and not her that tried that. Every one of us would have done the same thing if our Mother had of stopped three times to check on us, Susie told me. I couldn't laugh then but now it is really funny what Susie said and she is right. I think everyone felt bad for us, but was glad it wasn't them. Oh, this is too funny. My heart doesn't hurt anymore and I can just picture us laying there with everyone looking at the trailer with us zombies in it. Oh, my eyes are leaking. I am laughing so hard. My calf is going to think I'm crazy," said Gwenie.

"Ouch! My calf is washing the tears off my face," I said laughing. "Rough tongue; Wow; like sandpaper."

The calves knew something was not quite normal as we laughed and the tears rolled down our cheeks. They crowded around and licked our faces as we tried to comb them. Jeff sat on the ground and his calf lay down beside him with his shoulder in Jeff's lap. We just laughed harder, as Jeff said, "heavy, heavy." Lucy could not understand the laughter so she undone her gate and the calf pasture gate and came in to join us all. George and all the other horses followed her in. Trying to comb the calves with the horses wanting our attention was impossible. I called a stop to combing and got Lucy and the other horses, including George to follow me back to their pasture. Gwenie took my comb back to the shed with our brothers. They waited for me to close the gate and we all walked to the house together.

"You know, this could make an excellent speech for the 4-H speech competition as we could walk them through the stages and make them laugh," said Alan.

"I think it would take a while before I could tell this story without crying," said Gwenie.

"I think I am really tired. I think I can sleep now. This afternoon I thought I might never sleep again. I couldn't get my mind to stop circling. Now it just wants to laugh," I said.

"I'm more than ready to fall asleep too," said Jeff. "Me too!" said Alan and Gwenie together, as we laughed.

We all walked into the empty house. We removed our boots, coat, and hats, and walked up the stairs together. We thought Mom and Dad might be back in from the barn to tuck us in bed, before we finished brushing our teeth and saying our prayers. There was no sign of them yet so we each crawled into our own beds and called out goodnight. There was silence from Alan for a couple minutes and then we were laughing again. Alan was saying goodnight to us and the calves, the horses and the pigs. He was naming them all till laughter took over. "Topaz, Diamond, Emerald, Sapphire, Mr. Smith," he said before he started laughing.

8

FRESH MYSTERY

"Good morning," Mom called from the base of the stairs.

"Good morning," Jeff called, followed by Gwenie, Alan and I.

"My clock says it is ten minutes after eight," Jeff called out in a shocked voice.

"Yea," Alan called out, "my pillow had me in never-never land." making us all laugh.

Dad was standing beside the counter, where he sat down two cups of coffee and hugged Mom as we all descended the stairs and walked into the kitchen.

"Good morning." Dad said as we all crowded into them for hugs.

"Last night we were just loading all the Kopple's clothes into Grandpa Lorne's van so we can get them back clean and we could hear you all laughing, from your rooms. It was not fifteen minutes later we came up to tuck you in bed and you were all sound asleep," said Mom.

"What was so very funny last night?" Dad asked. "Alan thought he should say goodnight to us and all the animals, naming them one by one," Jeff said.

"Never a dull moment here," said Dad laughing.

"Breakfast is ready," said Mom, "just beseated. We have scrambled eggs, sausages and hot cakes this morning."

"Oh, my favorite," we all said together, including Dad. *"Heavenly Father, we thank you for this beautiful day you have given us. Bless us and all our families, friends, loved ones and neighbours. Lord, use us to do your work and guide our hands, hearts and mouths to your honor. Bless this food to our body's use, in Jesus name we ask, Amen,"* prayed Dad.

"Great breakfast," said Dad, as he pulled Mom into his arms and hugged and kissed her.

"You have to leave some hugs for us," said Alan.

"We will never run out of hugs," said Mom, "just like Great Grandpa and Great Grandma you will see today. It has been two weeks tomorrow since you have seen them so expect big hugs," said Mom smiling.

"Thank you for breakfast. Love you," said Jeff, as we all talked over ourselves, repeating the words.

"You are welcome and I love you too," said Mom.

"Love you more," said Dad.

"We love you more," we all said together.

"Let us see what our Bible readings tell us today. *It is Psalm19:14: Let the works of my mouth and the meditation of my heart Be acceptable in your sight, Oh, Lord, my strength and my redeemer.*

"What does that say to you?" asked Mom.

"Never say or think bad things about anyone. Pray for them that their life choices might strengthen their walk with the Lord," I said.

"Does anyone have anything to add to that?"

"I think Jackie said everything summed up. We just had this discussion two weeks, maybe three weeks ago at Sunday school," Jeff said.

"Great, now, I am going to finish doing lunch, for we will have company. Lucy decided to spend the night with the calves, so Dad triple-locked the gate on them this morning. We need you to do the chicks, turkeys, and laying hens in the old barn, your calves and Lucy's treats, please. Maybe she will go back to her own pasture, after treats. Then we can head over to the Kopples. We are going to set the house back so when they walk in nothing is out of place. It will just smell clean and fresh. You will see the hidden rooms and I just cannot imagine the surprise for the Kopples when they come home. We have invited both sets of parents secretly and we are going to have a surprise house warming party for them next Saturday afternoon, so everyone can see the hidden rooms in their elegant home, and then we will go to the hall for early supper party."

"Okay, rooms? Did you say hidden rooms?" Alan asked.

"Chore time, bye," Mom said laughing.

"Not fair," said Gwenie, laughing as she finished putting the cooking cutlery in the dishwasher, and headed for the mud room, behind the rest of us.

"Mom, can I make more ice in all the containers? Great Grandma loves our homemade ice cream and Lorrel will be here too, right, to help turn the crank," said Jeff.

"That is a great idea. Please do that. Thank you," said Mom.

Three of us walked to the old barn to start on the chores. The chick and turkey pens were finished by the time Jeff walked into the barn. Gwenie collected the eggs from the laying hens. I filled the water and feed containers as Alan and Jeff scrapped the floor into the grate. The milk cow stall had very few cow pies, which Jeff forked into the grate. I washed all the waste down the grate as those three went up to the loft. Lucy stuck her nose on my cheek. It made me jump. I turned and asked her, "what are you doing in this barn? I hear you had to console the calves las night. Hey, your gate was supposed to be triple locked I was told so how are you here?" George did not like the tone of my voice so he started braying very loudly. He was throwing his head in the air like a wolf or coyote and making an ear splitting noise. "George, you be quiet or I will turn this hose on you," I told him. I turned the tap off and put my hands on George's face when he went to lift it to start making racket again. I petted him and he settled down. I picked up the basket of eggs with one hand and I walked beside George, hanging onto his halter. All the horses followed us. Leaving the eggs safely on the stairs, I fed all of them their treat and walked them back to their pasture, triple locking the gate, again. My siblings were standing in front of the old barn by the time I finished the eggs and had them put away. The calves were pushing against the fence, trying to get closer to us. Animals do have a personality of their own.

We went into the calf pasture and George started the braying again. I am sure he is scaring the chickens at Grandma Linda's with his racket. "George that is enough of that noise! You have had your treat," I called to him. George kept up the noise until we walked out of the calf pasture to put their combs away.

"Oh, Dad just blew the horn. We got to go." Alan said. He blew the horn again in Grandpa Lorne's van and walked to his truck. We were ready to go see this hidden room or rooms.

"Last one to the van is a rotten apple," Alan called over his shoulder as he ran to put the comb away and be first to the van.

"Well Alan, I guess you are the rotten apple. You were the first and last one to the van as there is only room for one passenger. Got you." said Jeff as he joined us and stepped into the truck where Dad was sitting behind the steering wheel.

We followed Mom and Alan down the road. It was another beautiful day with the sun shining on the mountains, making them stand taller. The land was all bathed in glorious sunshine. The landscape always changes enough to make you love every change in it. Snow, no snow, wild animals, gophers, frost, sunshine, and shadows caused by clouds, keeps your eyes searching for change. Dad stopped so we could watch three deer run across the land. They jumped the fence and crossed the road in front of us and jumped the other fence heading for lands unknown. Or maybe they were going to go to the Highwood River to see how much ice was left. Oh, for the love of spring.

Dad turned into the driveway at Kopples where Mom was backing toward the house. The house was so beautiful back in the trees. It must have been the most elegant house in the whole country when it was built. It stood there shining and wet. Mr. McIntosh and Lorrel were pressure washing all the bugs and grime off the exterior. You could see the spray on the East side of the house occasionally sparkling in the sunshine. We crawled out of the truck, anxious to help.

"I will give you each one set of beautiful starched curtains, if you would take then upstairs to the bedrooms they belong in please, and we will follow with baskets and boxes of clean laundry, It will take a few trips but the curtains will be better for it." said Mom.

"Good morning Mrs. McIntosh, and Susie," we all said together as Mrs. McIntosh opened the door for us.

"Good morning and welcome to a clean smelling home, no smoke," Mrs. McIntosh said.

Susie scooted between us to get outside to go gather eggs, with the bucket she carried.

"What a world of difference a day can make," said Mom as she followed us in with Dad on her heels.

"You even had time to starch the curtains. Do you sleep?" asked Mrs. McIntosh.

"Jacqueline did all the curtains yesterday when we were here. The laundry was all finished when we got home except for our clothes and what we took home and the house was polished, the chores done, and supper ready. We are the most spoiled parents in the world," said Mom.

"Yes, I can see that. You have very hard working, loving kids," said Mrs. McIntosh, "and just like my two who are growing up away too fast. That speech Susie gave yesterday was just something else. Out of the mouths of babes, they say."

"She is an exceptional young lady, and a great help, at five years of age in eight months," said Mom laughing, joined in by us all.

"Mr. McCarthy, could I ask you to hang all the drapes as you can reach, please," asked Mrs. McIntosh.

"Consider it done, Madam," said Dad smiling. "Jacqueline, please bring the roll of drawer liner and scissors, lying just behind the driver's seat. That pretty paper in the dresser drawers will look great and smell pretty when we put the clothes back in," Mom said.

"Help! Help!" came screams from the chicken pen.

We all went out the door and bounced down the steps to the rescue. We watched Mr. McIntosh race to the pen and lift Susie up in his arm. Susie was clutching the basket of eggs as the rooster was trying to fly up to peck her legs.

"That bad rooster wanted to keep all the eggs for his chickens, and I didn't touch the ones where the two hens are sitting on a dozen each," said Susie.

"Maybe, we should put that rooster with his bad attitude in a pot for Sundaysupper."said Mr. McIntosh .

"Let's get back to work. We have company coming soon," said Mr. McIntosh who disappeared behind the house as we hurried toward the house.

The house smelt so fresh and even the air in the farm yard was fresh. The dog barked acting like it was going to escape and eat us. It quit the barking and played with what was left of a blanket in the enclosure. I juggled the roll of paper and scissors with my arms full of curtains. Many trips later, we had all the laundry in the house. The drawers were lined with paper and filled with clothes. The beds were all made and the rest of linen put away. The men were out pressure washing the exterior of the house. Jeff and Lorrel carried two carpets out of the house that were steam cleaned but still not real clean. Mr. McIntosh turned the pressure washer on them and the dirt disappeared, leaving soft colours showing. Jeff and Lorrel went into the house and brought out three more carpets. They turned out beautiful. Mr. McIntosh turned off the pressure washer and Dad curled up the wand hose. We could hear a vehicle coming up the lane. Everyone went out to meet the car. Hugs were shared by all and laughter rang out when Susie asked if they would be her Great Grandparents too. Great Grandma told her of course they would as we were all still laughing. "We always have room for more," she said. Her eyes sparkled as she turned to the house and said let's go see how it fared. It was priceless watching Great Grandma appreciate the beauty of the palour and living room, again. They had been invited to a party shortly after Great Grandpa built this house.

"Jacqueline, since you were the one who washed that book, go push on it," said Dad laughing.

"Wow, I love it," said Great Grandma, "what an elegant room. Check out that furniture. Oh, they have to sell it. They cannot let the babies crawl and chew on those pieces of furniture. They must have thought they were royalty, buying that furniture."

"Let's go upstairs," said Great Grandpa, "I have a surprise for you all. I just thought about it in the wee hours of this morning, while I was watching my beautiful bride sleep. My beautiful bride of nearly sixty years, and still as pretty as the first day I laid eyes on her." Taking Great Grandma's hand and kissing it made Great Grandma chuckle, shaking her head, and saying. "He took one look at me and his innards turned soft and they have never changed in nearly sixty years."

Everyone climbed the beautiful circular staircase and checked out the workmanship of the stairs and the house. Great Grandpa was so proud to tell us it looked as good as the day he built it. He walked over to the closet door and opened it.

"Oh, someone built shelves on the back wall. Jeffrey, will you go down to the trunk of my car and bring up the drill with that package of screwdriver bits please?"

"Yes Sir, on my way," Jeff said as we followed.

"There has to be a latch to open the trunk here some-where," Alan said, as he searched the dash and glove compartment of the car.

"Well I got it, with the key. The square key starts the car and the round key opens the doors and the trunk. Let's take the extension cord too. If we need it, we will have it and save us a trip back to this car." Jeff said.

Thank you, was said when we appeared at the closet with the tools.

"Now do you want to remove the shelves from the door, or would you like your Dad to do it?" asked Great Grandpa.

"We got this. We boys will take turns holding the shelves, catching the screws and undoing the screws. We will have those four shelves off in the shake of a rabbit's tail." said Alan.

"A sliding door with a secret compartment and stairs going down, Wow!" said Jeff .

"Oh, Stop, Please. It is absolutely full of spider webs. Let me grab the vacuum cleaner and clean it before you tract dirt and dust all over the house. I will hurry, ten minutes maybe. How about a cup of tea? I brought some special tea and you can relax while we ladies clean this up. This space is full of fresh air, no smoke. I love it," said Mrs. McIntosh.

Mrs. McIntosh and Mom stayed upstairs as we went to the dining room. I put the kettle on to boil. I found the tea pot and cups. Gwenie came out of the dining room with the tea cart.

"We will serve them like royalty," Gwenie said, making us laugh. Finding tea, cream and sugar in Mrs. McIntosh's box on the counter, we loaded up the tea cart. We also found bottles of soda pop. She had thought of everything.

"Will someone bring two light bulbs up here, please? They are in the bottom drawer of the cabinet closest to the door," Mrs. McIntosh called from upstairs. "Then ten more minutes and we will let you come up to see."

"Coming," called Susie who had the drawer open and light bulbs out before her Mom stopped speaking.

"This is excellent tea," said Great Grandma. "What a nice idea. How much work is left to do here?"

"I used Mr. McIntosh's pressure washer to clean the living room carpet that did not come clean being steam cleaned twice. It came out beautiful, which is drying along with the lounge drapes and I have a kitchen runner to pressure wash and I think we can call that finished, unless you find us more work in more hidden rooms," said Dad.

"We will see," said Great Grandpa. "Okay, you kids, walk up the stairs and follow the ladies down the secret stairs. Be very careful and we will follow you. You might be in for a surprise. Don't be leaning on any walls okay?"

"I feel like pouting. All this work and we have to wait to see the secret. Not fair," said Mr. McIntosh laughing, causing us all to laugh as we climbed the stairs.

We took our turn going into the closet. A long hallway in front of us had beautiful paintings hanging on both sides. Gwenie stopped in front of one painting.

"I could follow this dirt pathway and walk right around the corner in the tall trees. This artist is amazing," Gwenie said.

All the paintings were amazing and they were hung on both sides of the walls. The hallway was thirty six inches, (ninety two centimetres) wide. The stairs was a regular staircase with painting hanging above it descending to the bottom. With the anticipation of what we would fi nd below, we did not tarry long. We slowly followed behind Susie who went down the stairs like lightening.

Great Grandpa pointed to a hook high up on the wall a few feet inside the closet. "Not this minute, but if you turn that hook, a stair case will unfold from the ceiling to let you into the attic."

Everyone carefully walked down the stairs into a narrow room. The wall in front of the staircase had a cabinct of racks holding bottles of wine. Under the stair case was more racks filled with wine.

"The folks that had me build this home, took a vacation on a ship back to England and Scotland. That was more than eleven years ago. The Mrs. picked up some virus and they could not cure her. She had to stay there to get special treatments. Her husband traveled back and forth for a few years. They tried to sell this place for top dollar but the smell of all that cigar smoke, kept so many folks away. The husband traveled back to Scotland where he got sick, so he is with his wife. The Kopples decided they could make a living here when they lowered the price again. Looking at this art work, I think they will pay down the mortgage by more than half, if I know my art," said Great Grandpa.

"Wine racks. I forgot about all the wine racks. Wow, there is some well-aged British wine. I would say more than eighty bottles. Now see that hook. Turn it to the left and see what happens." laughed Great Grandpa.

The wall moved out and then slid sideways along the inside wall. We all walked in to a billiard room. A huge table covered in red velvet on the inside with all carved wood around. The legs were bigger than my waist and all carved. High back red leather chairs sat along the wall in two corners. Small round tables were between them. One table had crystal chess game on it. Paintings hung on the walls around the room. A cabinet against the other end wall held balls and above was a rack holding twelve pool cues. Everyone just stood and stared at the billiard table.

Great Grandpa escorted Great Grandma to one of the red leather chairs and he sat across from her. He told us if we wanted to go check out the attic, he would sit a spell.

Susie was the first one out of the room and up the stairs. We all walked out of the closet so Dad could turn the handle for the staircase to fold down out of the ceiling.

Susie came running with two flashlights and yelled, "me first." Her father told her he was going first to check the floor that it was solid wood and not just attic insulation. We waited and were called up to solid wood floors. The walls were not finished. Two dormer windows let light and sunshine in the empty attic.

"There is no treasure chest for us," complained Susie. Everyone laughed as we came out of the attic. Dad folded the stairs back into the ceiling. The boys stood the shelves along the side of the closet with the screws in a jar beside them. Lorrel said we should run to the basement and see where and how to get into the secret room. There was nothing unusual in the basement lounge area. Lorrel checked behind a painting, swinging it to the left and the wall slid forward and then slid sideways to reveal the billiard room.

"The painting, of course," Great Grandpa said.

"My dearest Love," Great Grandpa said to Great Grandma, "I would have built a house like this for you but we seemed to be so happy in our home with the memories of all our kids and grandkids and great grand kids. Are you still happy in our home?"

"Don't forget all your siblings, our cousins, friends, neighbours and customers. Your kitchen was the sunshine for so many folks," said Dad.

"We have the best home in the world and I would not change it for anything," said Great Grandma smiling up at Great Grandpa.

We all climbed the stairs and great Grandpa led the parade to the vehicles for the short trip to our home.

9

Hoist and Saddle Tree

"Mom if you want to take the van, and all our hard working cowboys and cowgirls, Mrs. McIntosh can follow in their truck and Mr. McIntosh and I will finish the carpet and we will behind you shortly. I can smell lunch from here," said Dad laughing that made everyone join in.

Great Grandpa led the parade to our home. We got into the van and closed the beautiful sunshine behind the windows. The sun shining on the mountains made them look taller with their crown of snow. The promise of spring was in the air. Susie was talking about how disappointed she was not to find a treasure chest. She said her house would have one. We were all laughing when Mom stopped at our house. By the time we washed and set the table, lunch was ready.

Jeff cooked the mixture for the ice cream before he seen the truck pull into the yard with the dads.

"Hungry men, they are here already," said Mrs. McIntosh.

"Hello," both dads called at the same time as they stepped through the archway with clean hands and faces."

Great Grandpa said, *"Heavenly Father, we thank you for this beautiful day we can spend it with our families and friends. Thank you Lord for all our blessings you bestow on us. Thank you Lord for the opportunity you gave to help a neighbour. We give you thanks Lord for this bounty we are about to receive. Bless each one of us and all our family, friends, loved ones and neighbours, and help us be your obedient children. Bless this food to our bodies use. We ask this in Jesus' name. Amen."*

Everyone was quiet as we helped ourselves to the lunch and passed dishes around. Great Grandpa started reminiscing. I can still picture this dining room the way it was when we finished building it. It was much smaller and filled with the same love. I was working on digging the root cellar in the side of the hill, where it still is now. I built the doors out of a fur tree that was so big, there was only one seam to glue together with the wood dowels we used. Let me tell you about wood dowels. They are round pieces of wood. When you want to put two pieces of wood together, you drill matching holes into the edge of both pieces of wood, as deep as your thumb. You cut the dowels a little less than double the length of your thumb. I remember I drilled six in each of the two doors. You put some glue on the dowels and push them deep into one side of the door. You run glue down the edge of the wood and onto the dowels that are sticking out. You line up the other half of the door and push them together with the dowels buried inside. You clamp the door tight together until the glue dries.

While I was doing this, your Great Grandma was in the yard scrubbing our dirty clothes on the washboard. The tub of water for washing was beside her so my young lady could enjoy the sunshine. Our horses and milk cow started running around their paddock. Out of nowhere came this noise. It was louder than a grader digging rocks on a hard packed road at a fast speed. The sky went dark to the northwest. The wind came circling around real strong. Your Great Grandma came running like lightening to the paddock. It was tough going but we managed to drag our animals into the root cellar with us. The sky went black. The noise was deafening. The rain came down like golf balls pounding everything. We had our hands full for hours trying to settle our animals. Great Grandma started to laugh.

Okay it was ten minutes and the noise was gone and the rain lightened up. We walked out into a strange world. I had to unwrap the wire gate that was all tangled in the paddock fence before we could lock our animals back in. To this day, we have never found the ramp for the chicken coop. Their building which was half tack room and half chicken coop was still standing undamaged. This window here in the dining room was much smaller and shattered.

Broken glass and hail was littered all over the table and
floor. Most of the laundry was caught in the fence where
I built your grandparents new house. Now that tornado;
you guessed it was a tornado.

It picked up trees, some as wide as this table, and
dumped them all over in your sheep pasture. It tore all
those trees out of the ground like pick-up-sticks. There
was not a large tree standing from the root cellar to your
cabin in the meadow. It jumped over all the trees here
just so you had somewhere to build you tree house,
before it sat down again further east. Everyone started to
laugh. It sure saved me a bunch of hard work clearing the
farm land. It took me two years to saw all those trees up
into lumber with my brother's help. I married the best cook
in the world. She kept us clean and fed. We built the old
barn out of some of those trees. We burned all the roots.
Funny thing is, if it happened nowadays, we could have
washed and dried those tree roots and made funny coffee
tables and such with them.

"Thank you for all the beautiful stories Great Grandpa,"
said Susie which made everyone laugh as she is just the
neighbour. "May we be excused, please? There is a barn
full of chicks and turkeys that I haven't seen yet and thank
you for such a delicious lunch."

"Would you like dessert?" asked Mom.

"May we come in before chores start and have dessert,
please?" asked Susie, looking around the table at all us kids.

"We need to make ice cream," said Jeff, as he picked up his dishes for the dishwasher, followed by us five.

"Shall I plug the tea kettle in for you?" I asked as everyone was helping remove the adults' dirty dishes to the dishwasher.

"Please and thank you," said Mom.

We all said thank you for lunch, as Jeff poured the cooled ice cream mixture into the ice cream churn. We added ice and rock salt around it and took turns cranking the handle. In less than half an hour, we had the ice cream ready. Jeff shared the licking of the beater with Alan and Lorrel. We all left the house with ice cream cones, stacked high with vanilla ice cream. Great Grandpa said he would share the huge tub of ice cream with the other adults. We reached the old barn before we finished our cones. We were watching the baby turkeys. As soon as our cones were finished, Lorrel asked if we could ride a horse.

"Sure," said Jeff as he looked at me and said let's saddle up and go to Grandpa Lorne's and bring back six more horses in case everyone else wants to ride.

I asked the rest to give the birds clean water and feed. I changed my mind and asked them to do the chores. We know how Susie loves gathering eggs. We will be about fifteen minutes, I told them.

"Lucy, you stay in the pasture. We are just taking our four now. Mom will be out later to ride you. Topaz, Diamond, Emerald," I said as Sapphire was walking with her head over my shoulder, as I opened the gate. "To the barn for saddles girls," I said as I triple locked the gate to keep Lucy and the others in the pasture.

Jeff had Emerald saddled by the time Sapphire and I walked into the barn.

"Your saddle is on the host already," Jeff said as he put Topaz and Diamond in a stall and closed the gate. "Fifteen minutes and we will be back to saddle you, so be patient," Jeff said as he closed the stall door.

I lowered my saddle on Sapphire and unhooked the hoist, returning it back in the tack room, rotating the saddles to hook Diamond's saddle for when it was time to saddle her.

Tightening the cinch and putting the bridle on, I mounted and raced Jeff out of the barn and down the driveway to Grandpa Lorne's pasture. In no time at all, we chose the six horses we wanted and headed back to our barn with them.

"Wow, I have never in my life seen anything like this before. No work involved, no lifting. Wow!" said Lorrel, as he watched Alan put the saddle on Diamond.

This was an invention that Dad and Uncle Bryan had worked on in welding class in high school. The boys started with a frame that stood against the wall that came out with a huge oval that rotated by a chain. This is power operated like a garage door, but instead of it going up, it goes around in a large oval, which has enough trees to hold eight saddles. When you want to go riding, you move your saddle to the top. The hoist is mounted close by and you operate the power switch. You hook the saddle horn and lift up your saddle from the saddletree then extend it to the aisle. After you put the saddle blanket on your horse, you lower the saddle onto your horse and release the saddle horn from the hoist. You then return the hoist to the starting position and you're free to cinch up your saddle and if you're so inclined you can use the step to help you climb into the saddle.

It's a perfect mechanism to get the job done without any lifting. At fourteen years old and using the profits from selling their 4-H calves, Uncle Bryan and Dad designed and built two of these systems to give to their parents for a Christmas present. There are three oval saddle tree stands which can hold twenty four saddles in all, in our tack room, here. His parents have one in their barn, as well as our Grandparents.

Mom often said she can't figure out why they didn't patent this design and sell it since it's such a space and energy saving device.

The bridles are always removed, put in the specially made cotton bag with our horse's name on it and hung over their saddle. That way, each horse always has the bridle they like and became accustomed to. It's hard to find the perfect bridle for each horse.

Alan laughed at Topaz who was wanting to go before her saddle was firmly on her back. Cinching the saddle and putting the bridle on, Topaz moved as Ruby and Opal entered the barn.

"Okay Opal, your turn," said Alan.

10

Easy Lessons

"Alan, uh, well, uh, we have never riden before," said Lorrel.

"Okay, well none of us were born knowing how to ride; we all had to learn, so today will be the day you learn," said Alan.

"Lorrel, please bring Opal over here, to the mounting platform. Before you can ride a horse, you have to meet them. Slowly walk up to her and let her sniff you. I want you to tuck into her and let her smell you as you rub her neck and front shoulders. She will not bite you, I promise. Keep that up until you are very comfortable. You can pet her face as well. They love knocking hats off. Your cinch is tightened, which means your saddle is secure. Come on up on the step. Put your left foot in the stirrup, while your left hand is holding onto the horn of the saddle. Now swing your right leg over, dropping into the saddle. Setting the stirrups for your leg length is the next step. Take your feet out of the stirrups and drop them down. The bottom of the stirrup must be level with your anklebone. Put your feet in the stirrup and stand. Please check that you have clearance of the width of your fist between your seat and the seat of the saddle. Oh perfect; you are set to ride."

"Susie, bring Ruby over here to the mounting step, I said.

Ruby is licking my ear and her tongue is so rough," said Susie. "She is the tallest horse in the world."

Ruby is one of twelve Galiceno mares that Mom and Dad purchased. They came from Mexico. They are considered a small horse because they all are around twelve hands high. Dad's horse Kernal is sixteen hands high.

"Bring her here and we will get you mounted. She likes you. Stand in the saddle please? Okay, your stirrups are set perfect. You are about the same size as our second cousin and she was using this saddle last summer.

There are rules:

We never kick our horses.

We never have the reins pulled tight.

They are all trained by sound and our movements. They will move by our voice or body language.

Gee; go right.

Haw; go left.

Step; move on.

Whoa; stop.

Walk; Trot; Canter; Gallop; are all commands they understand and will move too.

Back; will have them backing up.

Easy; Stand; Wait; will keep them still or mostly still, they like to move.

Over; Quit; lets them know you are getting off.

Clucking; clicking or clucking of your tongue is used to have them increase their gait. A kissing sound works also.

"Lorrel, you can ride between Alan and Gwenie and Susie, you ride between Jackie and I," said Jeff.

"We normally train new riders in the paddock, but with Lucy still in there it will be easier to go down to the gate for the cattle and circle around the back and we will come out between the two barns and circle again, Okay?" I asked.

"Works for us," Alan said as Gwenie answered with a nod of her head.

"Ruby stopped," said Susie, disappointed.

"Susie, look at your feet. Are they both in the stirrups? Are you safe in the saddle?" Jeff asked.

"No, my right foot is not in the stirrup. Okay, it's in now and Ruby is walking again," said Susie.

"We chose Ruby for you as she just loves smaller kids and she will stop if she feels a change of weight or loose stirrup," I said.

"Great, I love this riding," said Susie.

We would ride down to the gate going into the cattle pasture. We would turn there and ride to the other fence, where we turned and rode up behind the old barn. We rode to the new barn and turned there between the granary and the silos and one more turn put us heading back to the cattle pasture. We reversed direction and had about twelve trips completed. The weather was perfect and our new riders were doing great.

"Can we go see some different country?" asked Lorrel. "Well, you two are doing so great, maybe we can ride down to Grandma Linda's and check the chickens while we are there. Does the saddle feel good for you?"

"Excellent," said Susie. "I think I was meant to ride and not walk. Look at all the time in my life I wasted to find out I belong on a horse."

Everyone was laughing as we turned back toward the house and driveway to the road. Turning west was the road that stretched into a wide trail that turned into a pathway winding among the trees to the mountains. This was even more breathtaking on horseback. The mountains give off their own smell of fresh that just pleasures your heart. We turned left to ride on the road to Grandma Linda's farm.

"If you are really comfortable, we can speed up a little," said Alan.

"Okay, now use the saddle like a rocking horse. Instead of bouncing at every step, roll with the saddle. Oh perfect: you two are doing great," said Jeff.

"Susie, you have to stay by my side at all times. If you run into a problem, I can rescue you before you fall or something," I said as Susie kept saying gee to Ruby.

"Grandma Linda has a mounting step. Raspberry and George used to live here with her. When she was going away for a week, we came and walked Daisy the milk cow back to our place to milk. Raspberry and George decided they were moving to our place permanently. Now Grandma Linda has to come to our place to ride but Mom and Dad says it is better she is with us in case of an accident." said Gwenie.

Everyone dismounted, using the mounting step. Susie got the egg basket and gathered two dozen eggs. The boys put water in the water trough for the horses and the wild animals to drink. We helped her wash the eggs and put them in cartons. Susie wrote the date on them, which we could not read, before we put them in Grandma Linda's fridge. The boys came in and we took turns having a drink of water out of the blue water cup. Walking back out into the sunshine, we mounted and rode up the road. There was time to spare so we rode to the corner, back to Grandma Linda's and then back to the corner where we turned to ride to our gate. Turning into our driveway, we could see our moms and dads standing around Great Grandpa's car. We noticed Mrs. McIntosh look kind of sick. Her face turned a funny color and it seemed her knees went week causing her to squat a little. She stood and stared at her baby on a horse all by herself. You could see her fear.

"Are you having fun?" Dad asked.

"We are invited out for supper tonight so we must leave. Save our hugs until tomorrow after church, and you all have a beautiful day," Great Grandma said.

"Thank you, we love you," our four voices said from atop of our four horses.

"Me too," said Susie, "and thank you for showing us all the secret rooms. That was just wild. You have to build me a house like that when I grow up."

"My great grandsons might," Great Grandpa said as he drove down the driveway waving goodbye.

"Can we go saddle your horses? We brought four more mares from Grandpa Lorne's place. We have forty-five minutes before snack and chores," Jeff said.

"Sure," said Dad "sounds like a plan."

"Mom, please don't turn green. These are the best horses and they are excellent teachers. You will be riding like a pro before we leave this afternoon, please Mom," said Susie, as her Mothers complexion turned from green to red.

"We grew up in the city. We had never really been on a farm until we bought the Cross place. We have never ridden. I am much better at helping on committees than working with animals. If you can handle a couple of real green horns, we would like to show our kids we are not too old to learn, as I can see they just found a new love," said Mrs. McIntosh.

"Lucy, Kernal, Amber and Onyx, go to the barn so we can saddle you," Jeff said as he undone the gate. "No Raspberry, Grandma Linda is not here yet. Next week. No

Garnet, next time we will get you," said Jeff as he closed the gate to the pasture, and triple locked it.

The adults were walking to the barn. Dad whistled and Kernal and Lucy galloped to the barn, followed by Amber and Onyx. We turned back to the road. Let us ride to Grandpa Lorne's farm and then to Grandpa Gary's farm so we can give the greenhorns some privacy. Mom and Dad are great teachers. Your parent's will be experts without even realizing they were taught. Maybe we can add some speed along the way.

As we turned into the driveway at grandpa Lorne's farm, we speeded up. Susie bounced in her saddle until she figured out how to rock with her saddle, again. We circled around the farm and headed over to Grandpa Gary's farm. Alan was showing off some of his trick riding skills. Susie kicked Rudy with her stirrup and told her to move. She left me staring after her for a moment. She yelled gee and nearly fell off when Ruby turned. Alan stopped performing and they all watched Sapphire in hot pursuit of Susie. When I said whoa to Ruby, Sapphire stopped too. I managed to keep Sapphire moving and Ruby stopped, even though Susie was trying to get Ruby to run. I grabbed the bridle on Ruby and took the reins.

"I am an excellent rider. I can hold my own reins," Susie said.

We rode back to the barn in silence with me holding Ruby's reins.

I brought Ruby to the mounting steps first so Susie could dismount. I turned so Sapphire could walk to the tack room with Ruby in tow where I slid off Sapphire to the floor far below. I undid the cinch on both horses before Lorrel and Jeff came to operate the hoist. In minutes we had Sapphire and Ruby unsaddled. I led them out to the sunshine with two combs in my hand. Susie took the comb and started combing Ruby. We were joined by the other four, with their four unsaddled horses. We basked in the beautiful sunshine, rubbing our horses down. Susie dropped her comb and walked toward the house.

"Oh brother. I am so sorry. She has to have her own way constantly or she makes trouble. I will comb Ruby," said Lorrel.

"We will all help. Do not worry about her bad behavior. We are enjoying our day. We have a cousin who comes to visit and she is much worse," said Jeff.

11

THE BARN

"Lorrel, we have time for a quick tour of the barn if you want, before snack," Jeff said.

"I would love a tour. I can't believe how fantastic that saddletree and hoist work. I would love to see what other surprises your barn holds. I have to see this root cellar your Great Grandpa was telling us about. What a story. It must have been so scary to live through that tornado," replied Lorrel.

You have seen these normal stalls for the horses. If you look up, you can see the closed trap doors we drop the hay down for them. On the other side here is the herringbone milk parlour which holds eight cows. We have six cows plus Grandma Linda's Daisy. They come through a door on the west side, closer to the back of the barn. They walk into the milking parlour and walk into their stanchions which you can see are on an angle. That puts their tails close to the pit below. See how strong their stanchions are with the steel piping. Mom or Dad wash their udders and hook up the milking machine to them. When they are finished, they back out of their stanchions circle around the pit and walk the same alley they came in from. The walls are all white metal sheeting, as that whole area has to be washed down after every milking, with hot water. Those pipes take the milk to the cooler in the cream room. The channel under those grates on the floor takes everything to the sludge pit.

"I never dreamed there is so much to a milking palour. We just buy our milk in bottles at the store. This is some impressive. There are no carrying buckets of milk. This is beyond belief. I love it. Hey, should I go check on Susie?" asked Lorrel.

"Susie is being supervised by Gwenie and Alan. No worries," I said.

Next here is the butcher room. It has a hoist that comes out into the middle of the aisle here. There are stainless steel tables, equipment and white metal walls to make it easy to clean. There is hot and cold water in here. This door inside here goes into a cooler. That is Kopple's cow hanging there. When it is hung the proper time, we cut it up here in the butcher room and wrap it in special waxed meat paper, and then off to the freezer.

"No kidding; wow; when you buy your meat from the butcher shop you never think of what it takes to get it there. What a setup with the least amount of lifting. Your Dad sure believes in hoists. You could go into the butcher business," said Lorrel.

Moving past the mounting steps, you can see the sliding door to the pasture. This pen is for any animals that need doctoring. Across the floor is the sliding door to the east. Beside it is the tack room you know how to operate. This hoist gives us freedom. Our rules are we cannot lift more than ten pounds. Our saddles weigh more, so with the hoist we can saddle and go. This room holds a locked cabinet containing vitamins, medicine and supplies for the animals. There is a set of bunk beds for when an animal has to be watched. Calving time can get busy. All our branding irons are hanging here. You have cattle. You know you have to burn your brand into their hide to prove they are yours. Next is the bathroom with shower.

"You have such a beautiful clean setup here. It is just so organized. I hate branding. I hate the smell of the burning hair on those poor little calves," said Lorrel.

"Talking about freedom with the hoist, I have a story. When Mom finished feeding me, when I was a baby, she went to check on Jackie. She found Jackie had awaken from her nap and slipped out the door. Dad found her walking out the barn door to get her horse. Her saddle was hanging on the hoist in the middle of the aisle. After Mom searched the whole house, she came out to find Jackie crying because she couldn't go riding, as Dad was trying to reason with her. She was not yet three. Two thirds up the outside doors in our house, you will see special locks. No accidents are allowed on this farm," Jeff said.

"That is one story you did not have to tell," I said.

"Susie took off one day when we still lived in the city. She walked down to the grocery store for some candy. We were still searching for her in the house when we got a phone call from the clerk, we knew, who worked there. She walked over three blocks and she was just two. That was scary." Lorrel said.

It is time for the root cellar tour. Great Grandpa sure knows how to tell a story. I never knew about the trees. This root cellar was all redone in cement to remain safe forever. Great Grandpa built this new barn, from Mom and Dad's blueprints before Jackie was born. He redid the root cellar at that time. Both the solid wood doors he built are still being used. Two doors keep a stationery temperature inside of fifty degrees Fahrenheit. (ten degrees Celsius) There is all new wiring. Flip that light switch and let us enter. That huge cooler holds our cheese. Those big wheels of cheese have to be oiled and turned every week. Some are aged five years. We store eggs, cheese, cheese curds and milk here sometimes, too. This cellar is twenty feet (six hundred and ten centimetres) by twenty feet. There are bins for vegetables and fruit. Those shelves are full of jars of jams, fruits, and jellies that have been preserved. That chest is full of blankets and booties. There are two large folded tables and a dozen folded chairs. That cabinet has dishes, cups, silverware and whatever in case of emergency. Just need the crock pot of food. There is a transistor radio in case of tornadoes. You walked past a tarp close to the first door we came through. That is a generator for backup power. It is out there so the exhaust goes outside.

"I have never in my life heard of anything like this, let alone seen anything like this. You can survive everything. There are just no words for how impressed I am. I am blown away. This is beyond wonderful," said Lorrel.

"If we hurry, we can do the upstairs yet," Jeff said.

Stepping into the loft, the first thing you see is the little square hay and straw bales. At times, they are stacked to the roof all the way to the end door. That huge door in the front of the barn opens and our bale elevator is pushed in. Cowboys unload the trucks or trailers and throw the bales on the bale elevator. The elevator is a frame that is about eighteen feet (five hundred forty eight centimetres) long. It has tires under it so it can be moved and an engine on the front to turns the wide belt. It has a crank to lift the one end up. When you start the engine, the belt just keeps circulating so the bales ride on an angle up to the loft. Cowboys up here grab the bales and stack them. Lots of labor is involved, but it is so convenient for feeding, as well as protecting the bales from weather.

Here is the egg station. It has a sink for washing the eggs. Holding an egg up to this light shows the insides are perfect. They are put in cartons on this counter and dated. We take them to the cream room. Next door is the bathroom with shower. This is our cream room. We have to put on these slippers to go into the cream room. This cream room has a totally washable ceiling and walls. It has an air purifier to keep dust out. No dirty clothes or shoes are allowed in here. Hairnets and rubber gloves are used when we work with the milk or cream. The milk from the cows comes up the pipes into this refrigerated tank. It is equipped with a paddle that keeps the milk stirred as it cools. If the paddle is turned off , the cream will come to the top. We take the milk we need and the rest is run through the separator. The skim milk goes into that tank. That tank has pipes going down stairs to the shed and dumps in the tank for the pig mash. The cream goes into this tank until it is pasteurized. We make the cream into butter, buttermilk, cheese, cheese curd and quark. This is the butter table and the coolers against the wall.

"This is unbelievable. Everything set up for the least amount of work and so beyond useful. I am just speechless. Perfect dairy products," said Lorrel.

We rode past the silos. One is for the pigs and one for the dairy cows. The cows have a measured amount of grain that drops in their bowls as they get milked. There is a dial in the shed to measure the amount of grain for the pigs, according to how many we have. The floors can all be washed and if it gets bad, the bob cat can clean it up fast.

"Let us go check out snack time," said Jeff . "It is my favourite time of day."

"Snack time at your house is my favourite time of day too," said Lorrel laughing.

Gwenie, Alan and then Susie slid down the fire pole at the tree house.

"If there is time after snack I just have to check out your tree house. It looks like a cabin in the trees. I have never seen anything like it," said Lorrel.

"Jeff designed it and they built it in one weekend. It has everything. We have to have one at our farm," said Susie as we walked to the mud room.

Susie was the first one to use the boot jack. A boot jack is a piece of wood about eight inches, (twenty centimetres) long, and four inches, (ten centimetres) wide. One end is square and the other end has a U shape cut out of it called a yoke. There is a two inch, (five centimetre) block fastened on the bottom behind the yoke. You put your foot and weight of your body on the square end. Put the heel of your boot of your other foot in the yoke and pull. Your foot slides out of your boot as you stand. Change places with your feet and your boots are off.

"You have to wash Susie. We are not allowed through the arch without clean hands and faces," I said.

Susie turned and went to the sink without saying a word.

"We have homemade apple strudel and buttermilk for snack? Wow. This is the best," said Lorrel.

"God is Great and God is good, and we thank God for our food. By God's hand we must be fed. Give us Lord our daily bread. Amen." we all prayed. "Both Mom and Dad have full time jobs so we do not get a lot of homemade baking. Our Aunt Lilah lives in the

little house on our farm and she is a great cook like our Mom but she doesn't bake. This is the best I have ever tasted," said Lorrel.

"Mom and Dad say we are not the most spoiled kids. They say they were growing up, with always homemade snacks after school and meals," I said, "never bread or cookies from the store."

"May I have some more buttermilk, please?" Susie asked.

"It is hard work learning how to ride, eh?" I said laughing as I filled everyone's glass again.

Great Grandpa Chester sure had some stories. We have never heard the story of the tornado. He built the barn where the chicks, turkeys and laying hens are, just before Grandpa Lorne was born. It was located where the granary is west of the silos. It had wood shakes on the roof and plank siding. Only a couple of poles have been replaced because a new mother cow was herded in the barn with a bunch of cows ready to calf. Her new baby was left hidden on the land. She let them know she wanted out by trying to bring the barn down. Grandpa and Dad let her out and she went right to where she'd hidden her new calf, so they were able to bring both inside out of the cold.

Great Grandpa built the new house where they live now. He bought the land that was solid trees of all sizes. He moved the sawmill and built a fantastic booming business where it still is today. The large trees were run through the sawmill and cut into lumber. Smaller trees were cut for logs, rails and fence posts. The fence posts were sharpened on one end, to a point. The bark was peeled off with drawing knives thirty inches (approx 76 centimetres) from the point. Painted with a product called blue stone sealed and protected the posts from rotting when in the ground. With his brothers and his children he got more into construction. Now he has more than thirty employees; carpenters, electricians, plumbers, fencers, cement workers and farmers. We will have to take you on a trip over there, especially if you need lumber for your tree house.

Grandpa Lorne bought this farm from him when he married Grandma Ella Katherine. He did more farming than working with the lumber, as he was farming this land, but like his brothers, they worked where they were needed. Grandpa remodeled this house and put green metal roof and red metal siding on the barn. He built the pig barn with lumber he sawed from the trees off this land. Mom and Dad bought this land from Grandpa Lorne before they were married. Great Grandpa's company built the new house for Grandpa Lorne, where we were today, then did this house so Mom and Dad could spend their honeymoon here.

That old barn was lifted off its rock foundation by great Grandpa's company and moved it over thirteen yards (twelve meters) to the west. They put it on a new foundation that was two feet (sixty one centimetres) higher allowing a drainage system to be installed under the cement floor.

It was then remodeled to hold new turkeys and chickens, as well as an area for the laying hens on one side of the long barn. The other side has pens to bring in new lambs and calves. You saw the large pen that holds the seven milk cows. We never showed you the wide door that has strips of thin rubber running from top of door to floor. This allows them to come and go as they please and not cause too much of a temperature change in the barn. The thin rubber strips are slightly overlapped, which keeps them in place in a wind storm. After they built the state of the art new barn, the tack room was moved to the new barn. The upstairs is full of straw and hay bales that are safely out of the weather and easy to drop through the trap doors.

"I don't think Great Grandpa will be able to build Susie a new home years from now but the company sure can, even with secret rooms," laughed Alan.

"Wow, what a life. Imagine, living on the land that your Great Grandpa owned when he was not much more than a teenager. No one anywhere in our parents' families farmed or lived anywhere but a city," said Lorrel.

"Hurry, let's put our dishes in the dishwasher. Mom and Dad are walking toward our truck," said Susie. "Dad is carrying a gallon of buttermilk. It looks like Mom has butter and cheese. Wow, we will eat like kings and queens, with fresh farm products. I love it," Susie said as she hurried out the door calling good bye, behind her, followed by Lorrel.

"Good bye," we all called as they ran out the door.

"Mom and Dad are going in the basement. Wonder what's up? Gwenie asked as we all headed to the staircase to the basement.

"Hello my little angels. We can all spend thirty minutes in the recliner chairs before we start chores, okay?" Mom asked.

"Hello," we all called as Dad ruffled our hair as we sat in our recliner chair.

Mom turned on the television. Mickey Mouse was on. "McIntoshs all loved riding. They will join us again. I told them we would help find horses and tack for them. They are learning fast to be country folks," said Dad.

"Wake up. It has been forty five minutes and Mom and Dad sneaked away and left us resting," Jeff said. "We only have the pigs, the sheep and our calves to do. It won'take long. I had a good nap. I feel really recharged now."

"Yes, I had a great nap," Alan said stretching. We hurried up the stairs to get our coats on. The boys fed the pigs while we girls fed the sheep. Our caves didn't like us riding today and giving our attention to our horses. What crazy animals. They acted like they have to compete for our attention. They tried to keep us from leaving their pasture by pushing against us when we tried to walk to the gate. After fifteen minutes we left to go see what we could fix for supper. The evening was showing us how beautiful it could paint the sky. The sun was still peeking over the mountains as the sky was turning dark blue, pink and gold. A cooler wind was blowing. Rather than standing and enjoying the sunset, we hurried into the warm house.

"Mom has two casseroles in the fridge but I think that is for the Church Social tomorrow. There is leftover turkey stew from yesterday, which we can mix with the chicken stew we had today for lunch and we can serve that on toast with coleslaw salad.

Does that sound like a plan?" I asked.

"Excellent," said Jeff. "I think I would like chocolate pudding for dessert. How does that sound?"

"You are on. I am going to take our homemade ice cream out of the freezer and put it in the fridge to soften. Um, hot chocolate pudding with a scoop of ice cream. Who needs supper?" said Alan laughing.

"I'll set the table," said Gwenie.

"I will get the salad and do the toast," said Alan.

"The pudding is thickened and I see the stew is hot," said Jeff. "That did not even take fifteen minutes and I see Mom and Dad walking up from the barn. They have perfect timing."

"Hello," said Mom as she walked into the kitchen. "I believe I am really short on my quota of hugs today."

"Hello," we all said as we crowded around for hugs.

"Me too," said Dad, as he joined in for hugs.

"Heavenly Father, thank you for this beautiful day we had. Thank you for our beautiful kids with their hearts of gold, and my wife who gives them their beautiful

looks. Thank you for all our friends, neighbours, family, loved ones. Bless us all that we might walk this earth with you front and center in all our thoughts and deeds. Bless this food to our bodies use. We ask in Jesus name, Amen." Dad prayed.

"Do you want television tonight or is it time we all had a quiet evening with our books?" asked Mom.

"I think we tried Mickey Mouse and went into dreamland so I am game for an evening in my room," I said laughing.

"Me too," was answered by everyone else, including Dad, which made everyone laugh.

"One of these days we are going to have a leisurely day and we will get the games out and spend an evening playing games, if that is at all possible. It seems every day it gets busier and it won't be long till the calves start to come and Spring work will start," said Dad.

"Well, if we didn't have to waste so much time going to school, we would have more time to help out and more time for fun," said Jeff .

"Why don't you help put the dirty dishes in the dishwasher and bring your fantastic looking hot chocolate pudding so I don't have to give you the same old lecture about going to school and college," said Dad.

"I have the ice cream and the ice cream scoop," Alan said.

"Delicious supper, thank you," said Mom.

"Yes thank you all so much," said Dad. "Now off to your rooms and we will be up soon to tuck you in bed.

12

ELK, DEER, COYOTES

"Good morning," Jeff called as he turned off the alarm, which was set louder than usual.

"Good morning," I called, with Gwenie and Alan, echoing the greeting as they were crawling out of their beds, also.

We all walked to the feed shed together. Gwenie and I got the pails of feed for the baby turkeys and chicks, as Jeff started the garden tractor and drove out of the shed. Alan closed the door. We met back at the shed. Jeff drove the tractor with trailer in as Gwenie and I grabbed the baskets to collect the eggs, and buckets of feed for the laying hens. The boys fed the sheep and went to the old barn to throw down the wedges of straw and hay. We met them there and we all walked to the pig barn together.

All the purebred Yorkshire feeder pigs had finished eating. We closed Mr. Smith's pen. Next was the four mothers; Ms. Dolly with fourteen piglets; Ms. Becky with sixteen piglets; Ms. Karie with thirteen piglets; and Ms. Charlotte with thirteen piglets. They were all in their special farrowing pens. Each pen has two compartments. The sow is on one side which is not wide enough for them to turn around. The piglets have a narrow pen with the bottom board removed so they can come under and suckle. Piglets need a safe retreat to avoid being squashed under their mother who are not careful at all where they drop down to sleep.

"Oh look," said Gwenie. "Ms. Dorry is acting funny."

"You bet," Jeff added.

"The calendar says she is due to have her piglets next Tuesday," Gwenie said.

"Oh well," I said. "They'll come today I think so let's put some bedding in both the farrowing pens and we'll put her in next to Ms. Dolly. We might as well put Ms. Summer in too. Dad will check them later and let her out if she isn't ready."

"We still have ten minutes, so let's go brush our calves," I said.

"Yes", Jeff replied, as he finished shutting gates in the pig barn.

Ten minutes of brushing our calves left them wanting more of our attention. Lucy watched us leave the calves. She opened the gate and led the eleven horses and George to the barn.

"We have time for our shower and put on our church clothes before Mom and Dad come in," I said. "Gwenie, you can shower first. I will make fresh coffee and be up behind you.

Alan and Jeff tried to beat Gwenie up the stairs, with all of them laughing.

We all returned to the kitchen sparking clean in our Sunday best clothes.

"Here comes Dad in Grandpa Lorne's van. I thought he was waiting his turn for the shower with Mom. Maybe we can enjoy a longer breakfast this morning," said Gwenie.

"Good morning Dad," we all called when he entered the kitchen, getting in line for hugs.

"Mom is in the shower, and your coffee is ready if you want to join her," said Jeff.

"Love you all. I will go up and shower and get all dolled up for church. You all look great. I don't suppose you will just relax," Dad said, as he headed for the stairs with two cups of coffee.

We put on aprons with bibs that covered the front of our church clothes. Only Sundays would we be bothered with aprons. We took the bacon and eggs out of the fridge. I mixed up the batter for the French toast. Jeff cooked the bacon. Gwenie cooked the eggs. I soaked the bread in the batter and cooked the French toast. Alan set the table.

"I just love your menu. You realize, you are the best children in the world," Mom said. "I love you."

"I love you more," said Dad as we all sat at the table with the hot dishes in front of us.

"Heavenly Father, thank you for this day you have given us. Thank you that we can go to your house and worship with your children and have fellowship today. Bless us and all our families, friends, neighbours and loved ones. Lord, direct our hearts and mind to do your work, by being with us always, guiding us. Bless this food to our bodies use. We ask this in Jesus' name. Amen" prayed Dad.

"This chokecherry syrup is so great on the French toast. I think I like it better than our maple syrup," said Alan.

"Yea and it was so much fun picking the berries and making the syrup. We have to pick again this year, and if the bears don't eat all the huckleberries, maybe we can go up the mountains and pick some this year, too. I can just taste huckleberry syrup on my French toast," said Gwenie. "We can ride up there with George carrying the buckets for picking and he can carry the berries home for us. Maybe Uncle Bryan, Aunt Brenda, Annette and Douglas can come with us this year. Of course, Grandma Linda will come, as Raspberry will not be left out."

"That is a plan. We will pack a picnic lunch and make a day out of it. It could be as much as ten mile trip by the time we get home. An excellent summer outing," said Mom, smiling at Dad.

"Fifteen minutes to departure time. Thank you for breakfast," said Dad, as we all put the dirty dishes in the dishwasher.

With smiling faces and brushed teeth we joined the casseroles, milk, buttermilk and butter that were loaded into the van. Obeying the rules, we quietly sat for the eighteen minute trip to church. To get into the proper mood for church, everyone has to just sit back and meditate on the scenery and the service to come. The only quiet minute from dust to dawn Great Grandpa Chester tells us.

More ducks had joined the others on the frozen pond; they had found more weak spots and had water coming up over the ice. The roads were dusty. Searching for more signs of spring didn't bring much change since yesterday. The Kopple house gleamed through the trees as Dad drove past their driveway. Cattle were out in the pasture pushing each other around the hay bales. Equipment was in the farm yard where the house had burnt down last fall. One more turn and Dad drove in the church parking lot. There was already about twenty vehicles parked. Some folks were walking in the church while others were carrying lunch into the hall. Great Grandpa's company built this new hall about six years ago. The old one had no indoor plumbing, kitchen or coat room and was too small.

One of our Sunday school teachers was away so every one older than nine sat in the same class. The teacher made it entertaining with lots of laughter as she got the lesson across. We sang five songs during the Church service of faith and hope for the future.

Everyone went to the hall after the last prayer. We lined up to the buffet table after the blessing and filled our plates. The adults all sat around five round tables. The boys pushed three rectangular tables together. The older boys sat at one end and jumped into helping Lorrel design his tree house with the measurements he brought, after they finished dessert. We girls sat at four tables and supervised and fed the six little ones in highchairs. We tried to design dresses we would wear to the June social. Judy, who was seventeen, brought a magazine that was full of city clothes from New York. We decided that not one outfit could be worn to the pig barn without scarring them. New York City does not know beautiful western clothes.

We had laid the smallest kids on their blankets in the coat room. Only forty minutes passed before one woke up and woke the others up. It was nearly three o'clock. What an enjoyable day. We left the tables set up for the Kopple party next Saturday. With empty dishes and jugs, we walked to the van.

"Did you have a good time?" asked Mom and Dad together that got us all laughing.

"Susie entertained us being smart and funny. It was nice to visit with all our friends and we were planning projects," said Jeff as we all said what a fun day it was.

"What is your Bible verse today?" Mom asked.

"Oh, that was a long time ago. Wow. We might need a minute," I said laughing.

"Psalm 19:14: Let the words of my mouth, and the meditation of my heart, be acceptable in your sight, O Lord, my strength and my redeemer," we recited together.

"Excellent," Mom said. "You have ninety minutes, until chore time to relax or do as you please, at home."

"Thank you," we all answered as we checked out the country side.

Before long we were home and got out of the van to change into our barn clothes.

Fifteen minutes later, we had our four horses saddled and were riding out of the barn.

Riding out of the driveway, we turned to Grandma Linda's farm. After checking the chickens and filling their feed and water dish, we opened the gate to the half section of land to explore for animals and wildlife.

"Look down in the coulee. There is a herd of mule deer, and a coyote is running along the top of the coulee. The deer are ignoring the coyote," said Alan.

"There is an elk up the end of this draw," said Gwenie pointing towards the draw.

"It is so beautiful here, we could ride till sundown but we better head back," I said.

The elk was not moving from where he was eating on the hillside. It watched us ride on the ridge above. It was so peaceful riding out there with no buildings or noise. We reluctantly turned toward home. Before we had our horses unsaddled, Lucy walked in the barn with all the others in tow. I locked them all in the stall until we finished combing our horses. I fed all them their treat before I walked them back to their pasture and closed their gate. I hurried to help Gwenie who was doing chores in the old barn.

The boys were at the pig barn. We joined the boys after they called to us. We love seeing the new babies born on the farm. Before long we finished chores and walked to the house.

"Hello," said Jeff, who was the first one to finish washing and step into the kitchen.

"Hello," said Mom and Dad who were in the kitchen preparing supper.

"You were faster than us doing chores," laughed Gwenie as she was next through the arch way.

"Did you all have a great day today?" asked Dad.

"Absolutely, it was the very best," we all answered.

"The calendar said next Tuesday we would have spring babies but we have them early. Ms. Dorry has blessed us with thirteen healthy piglets. Ms. Summer has chosen to give us with thirteen healthy piglets as well," said Jeff.

"Yes, we have checked on them, thank you. If you would like to set the table, supper is ready," Mom said.

We bowed our heads as Dad said prayer for supper.

"We didn't ride today but we had a beautiful day." said Mom. "I just love it when Spring is knocking on our door promising warmer temperatures and bringing the land back to life after the long winter sleep.

"We had a beautiful ride today. We went and done the chickens at Grandma Linda's and then we rode the west half section, checking out the coulee and draws. We saw mule deer, an elk and a coyote as well as birds," I said.

"Excellent," said Dad. "What do you want to do after supper?"

"Quiet time is good for me, please," I said.

"Yea, that sounds like a plan for me," said Jeff .

"Me too," said Alan and Gwenie at the same time.

"Do you realize, that it was not twenty minutes after you went for quiet time last night you were deep in dreamland," said Mom. "Maybe we are working you away too hard."

"Hardly," said Jeff , "It is the school work that wears us out," making everyone laugh.

"Okay, my little angels. We will be up after you finish your showers and teeth to tuck you in bed," Mom said, as Dad got up from the table and answered the phone. It was our ring. Grandma Linda and we are the only ones on this party line.

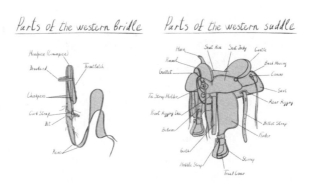

Parts of the western bridle   Parts of the western saddle

13

Cheese Curds

"Good morning," called Jeff as he turned his alarm off that seemed to be louder this morning.

"Good morning," Alan and Gwenie called. "Ring, ring, pause ring, came from the phone. I'll get that," I said as I bounced down the stairs to answer the telephone.

"Great Monday morning, good news," I said. "There was a water main break in town and the school street and grounds are flooded. Equipment is going to be digging up the road so Mrs. Jenkins phoned to tell us school is canceled today."

"Right on," said Jeff. "Guess what. We are out of buttermilk and with the Kopple's farm work and all; we need to spend most of the day in the cream room. I imagine we will make butter and cheese and maybe some quark and maybe we can do a new batch of ice cream. What a glorious day!"

"Fantastic," Gwenie said as she met everyone in the hall, heading for the kitchen.

"No school lunches today, Mom. No school. Mrs. Jenkins phoned and told us school was closed because of a water main break near the school." I said as Mom walked into the kitchen from the mud room.

"Yes, we know. Mrs. McIntosh called to see if Lorrel and Susie could spend the day here as they want to ride. Please set the table for two extra as I think I hear Mr. McIntosh's truck now. We have to work in the cream room today. I have the delivery truck coming today for an order of cheese, butter and cheese curds. Maybe you can take turns helping between riding, as Dad has to haul some grain today," Mom said.

"Mom, after breakfast, I will turn and oil the cheese before I start hauling grain," Dad said as he walked into the kitchen.

"Oh please, it is going to be a busy day, and with two extras asking questions, it will only slow the process, I'm afraid."

"We can gag Susie, if you want," said Alan, laughing. "I can take her with me for a trip if you like Mom." Dad said. "In fact, they both might want to come one trip to check out the country side."

"Come in," Dad called as he walked to the door. "Good morning," said Mr. McIntosh. "You really don't mind having extra company today?"

"No problem at all. We were just talking and I might take them one trip in the truck to haul grain, as it is cream room work today. Would you like to join us for breakfast? Kids, if you wash up, breakfast is nearly ready."

"Why thank you but I best get to work," said Mr. McIntosh. "Are you sure it isn't too much for you today?"

"Our house is usually full of extra family so two more is not a problem at all." You have a great day and we will see you later. You are joining us for supper tonight." "Thank you. We will be looking forward to this evening for sure. Have a great day. Good bye," said Mr. McIntosh. "Good bye and have a great day," Dad said again. "We ate cereal but if it is okay, we would like to eat again with you," said Susie. "It looks and smells so good." *"Heavenly Father, thank you for this beautiful day. Thank you for all our blessings. Lord, bless us and our families, friends, neighbours and loved ones. Lord, guide us to do your work with happy hearts. Bless this food to our bodies use, we ask in Jesus name, Amen."* Dad said.

"Do we have chores to do?" Susie asked. "Breakfast is excellent, thank you."

"All finished," I said. "Mom, what is your schedule? What can we do to be the most help?"

"Grilled cheese sandwiches for lunch okay?" asked Mom. "How would you like to do vegetables for a pot roast for supper? I will get the big crock pot and if you will please do garlic, onions, turnips, carrots, celery, potatoes, a package of peas and a package of corn, and set it on low for all day. The McIntosh's will join us for supper tonight. Maybe some hot biscuits with it, and chocolate pudding or rice pudding?" asked Mom.

"Perfect," said Dad, "I will get the beef, peas and corn out of the deep freeze. I am always so thankful that you freeze vegetables so we can enjoy our garden in winter and spring."

"Now Dad and I are going to go turn and oil the cheese before I go to the cream room. Susie and Lorrel, you can take a ninety minute ride in the big truck to get grain. You can come to the cream room to see how we wrap one pound packages of butter, after you are suited up. Next time you can help. The grain truck is parked beside the barn and you can all go to the truck after you finished filling the crockpot for supper. Then my four can come to the cream room. The delivery truck should be here at four o'clock for butter, curds and cheese. Latter, this afternoon you will be able to ride again for at least two hours, so it should be a great day for you, plus you can make home-made ice cream today, okay?" said Mom.

"Daily devotion is now," said Mom. *"Today we have 2 Corinthians 9:7 So let each one give as he purposes in his heart, not grudgingly or of necessity; for God loves a cheerful giver."*

"What does that tell you?" asked Mom.

"It says, with a happy heart, help and give without reservations," I said.

"Excellent, anyone else want to add to that?"

"I think that just about says it all," Jeff said.

"Excellent. Thank you for breakfast," Susie said as she jumped up and carried her dishes to the dishwasher, followed by everyone. "I am really good at peeling carrots."

"If everything is under control, Dad and I are going to the root cellar. I am so proud of you and all you can do to help. Please be careful, I love you all," Mom said.

"The smartest most helpful kids in the world, you are. Love you," Dad said as he walked under the arch with Mom.

"Thank you for everyone's help. We have everything in the crock pot and it turned on low, for the day. Did you bring your tooth brushes?" I asked.

"Oh, no," said Susie. "We never brought anything."
"Okay, here is a new toothbrush. Put your name on the handle with this permanent marker and you can put them in an empty cup in this cabinet. They will always be here for you and no one else will use them. We have to brush after every meal and snack," said Jeff.

"Thanks, you know you spoil us," said Lorrel.

We brushed our teeth and dressed for the outdoors. We walked toward the grain truck. The truck was running. Dad was not in the truck. We stood in front of the barn until Dad walked up behind us from the root cellar. In this yard, if any vehicle or equipment is moving, we are not. We stand safely out of danger until the vehicle or equipment passes or until it is shut off. We wait until we are acknowledged before we run toward a machine just shut off. Mom and Dad never want any accidents caused by not seeing someone. It really is a very easy rule to follow.

"Okay, my little angels please go help your Mother and my two precious passengers, let's go get into the truck," said Dad.

"Good bye," we all called at the same time.

"Hello Mom" we called through the door of the cream room.

"Hello, can I get you all to take the wagon and round up all our gallon jars. I think there are three in the house yet, and the rest will be in the root cellar. Please wash them again in the sink in the egg room and then get suited up and we can sterilize them here," Mom said.

"Okay, we called through the closed door as we turned from the door to hurry down the stairs.

We entered the cream room in white coveralls with our slippers and hair nets on, carrying the gallon jars to where we could sterilize them.

"Mom, we have twenty-six gallon jars, here." Jeff said.

"I have to maintain this temperature on the cheese curds for another hour," Mom said, "Could you put six gallon jars in the tray and run it through the sterilizer, please? I have twenty gallons of cream being churned into butter. That will give us a little over ten gallons of buttermilk and eighty pounds of butter. Now please let those jars cool before you stack sixteen of them in the cabinet. I don't want any burnt fingers as we have time before we extract the buttermilk."

"Who would like to wash down the inside of the cooler before we put the buttermilk in it?"

"Me," was answered by all of us, making Mom laugh. "Let's wash the butter cooler too, so how about the girls do one and the boys do another, okay?" I asked.

"All finished," Alan said.

"Us too," said Gwenie.

"Thank you it looks like about another twenty minutes till the butter is ready to work. You can play dice if you want," said Mom.

"Wow, twenty minutes goes really fast when we are playing dice," said Alan.

"Please bring the stool over to hold the gallon jars as I open the plug in the butter table to drain the buttermilk," said Mom.

"Okay, all that buttermilk is in the cooler," said Mom.

"Please squeeze the butter," Mom said as she kept stirring the cheese curds.

"Hello," called Susie, as she knocked on the door.

"Susie, your and Lorrel's coveralls are set on the shelf with hair nets and slippers. Please wash your face and hands before you come in," said Mom.

"It's just me, Lorrel has not figured out how to shift the truck perfectly in his mind yet so he is doing one more trip with Mr. McCarthy," said Susie.

Alan and Jeff burst out laughing, as they knew they have done the same thing. We joined in, laughing.

"Susie, first time in the cream room you sit in the corner, where the dice is and observe the entire goings on so you can help next time," said Gwenie.

"What are you doing?" asked Susie.

We are making butter. To make butter you first pour the cream into this rectangular stainless steel table. You turn the paddles on to churn the cream into butter. When the butter becomes really thick, we drain the buttermilk off through the plug here in the corner of the table. We then use these hand held wooden paddles to squeeze the rest of the buttermilk out of the butter. After we drain all the buttermilk, we replace the plug and put lots of cold water in the table. We use the hand held wooden paddles to squeeze the butter to get all the hidden buttermilk out of the butter. We drain this into the skim milk tank to make the mash for the pigs. We wash the butter twice more to make sure it is perfectly clean from buttermilk. The paddles are changed to ones that squeeze all the butter to the end of the table. When it is the proper height it is cut with the cutter instrument. Every pound of butter is wrapped in the butter paper. It is carried to the cooler, to cool.

"What are you cooking?" asked Susie

"I am making cheese curds. They are the best when they are really fresh," said Mom.

"You know my next question," laughed Susie.

"I heat the cream to ninety six degrees Fahrenheit (thirty five point five degrees Celsius) for ninety minutes. I add some product and cook another thirty minutes. I stir in product and let it set for thirty minutes. I cut it into three-quarter inch cubes. I heat the curds slowly bringing the temperature up to one hundred and sixteen degrees Fahrenheit (forty six point six degrees Celsius), for sixty minutes. I dump the curds into cheese cloth and let it hang for thirty minutes, to drain any liquid left. Next we put the curds in this colander here and I press it with eight pounds of weight for three hours. After three hours we break the curds mass into bite size pieces and toss in a bit of salt. We weigh out four ounce and eight ounce packages. We seal the packages and put our labels on them. The truck will be here around four o'clock today. It is a rush to get this done before the truck comes. Does that answer all your questions?" asked Mom.

"Yes, thank you. The butter looks so perfect in your packages, just like we buy in the store," said Susie, making everyone laugh.

Susie sat quietly while we wrapped the butter.

"Okay, eighty pounds of butter wrapped and in the cooler. There are ten and one half jars of buttermilk in the cooler. Now Mom can we take out the half jar and pour out a glass for each of us?" I asked.

"Absolutely, we need a little refreshment, before you little angels leave. As soon as you are finished your buttermilk, I will sterilize the butter table, all the paddles and do the cleanup. The cheese curds will let me take a break in forty-five minutes, too," said Mom. "Thank you for all your hard work."

"You are welcome," said Susie, "and thank you for the best buttermilk in the world."

"Yes, you worked so very hard, Susie," Jeff said, making everyone laugh.

"Learning is hard work. Next time I come in here I will know exactly what to do without having to ask questions. Now, I want to check out your tree house, again.

14

ATTITUDE

We left the cream room and took off our protective wear and folded it neatly for us to use again. Susie raced down the stairs and was off through the sliding door at the back of the barn. She rolled under the fence to the yard. When we arrived, she was trying to climb up the fire pole into the tree house. Giving up, she climbed the rope ladder.

"I love it. Oh, the floor is dirty and the windows are kind of spotted. Can we work on shining it up, now?" asked Susie.

"You didn't have enough cleaning at Kopples? Okay let's wash the windows and the floor, and shine it up, before we go make lunch," said Jeff.

Susie started singing some hymns from Sunday school and we joined in, as we cleaned.

"Look, there are rabbits in the garden. There are little baby rabbits," said Susie.

They are born early I think. We will have to take more vegetable peelings out to their tree house home, cheating the chickens out of some." I said.

"What tree house home?" Susie called from the fire pole she was sliding down.

"We have a family of rabbits so Dad dug a hole real deep into the hill and put some wood around it for a house. Dad brought a huge dead old tree with the middle rotted out of it for the front of the house. The rabbits can go inside the middle of the trunk and turn into their house."

"I will get the vegetable peeling from this morning and we can walk over to their home," said Alan.

"Hurry Alan, I want to see their house," said Susie

"Can I crawl in it? It looks like a pretty small hole," asked Susie.

"No," we all answered together.

"This is their safe haven. We cannot invade their privacy or they just might move away," said Gwenie.

"Let's go start lunch. Dad should be back soon and Mom should have the curds under the weight soon," I said.

"Dad is walking beside Mom, carrying a gallon of buttermilk. Lorrel is walking behind them. You are on the last sandwiches, aren't you, Jackie," Jeff asked me.

"Yes, lunch will be on the table by the time they wash," I said.

"Hello, you hard working little angels," Mom and Dad said together as they walked through the arch, making them and everyone laugh.

"Heavenly Father, we thank you for this beautiful day. Guide us to do our work safely. Help us and guide us to be your better obedient children as we learn daily of your love. Bless us, Lord and our families, neighbours, friends, and loved ones. Bless this food to our bodies use for your honour. We ask this in Jesus name, Amen." Dad prayed.

"Thank you for lunch. It was beyond delicious," said Susie.

"Lorrel, can you drive the big truck now?" asked Alan laughing.

"If I had to, I could do it. I know where to have the wheels to make corners and twists and turns. I know what rpm to shift loaded and empty. I think if it was an emergency, I could do it, at my age without my license." Lorrel said.

"That is so nice to know. Now I have the choice of three boys to call on if I need a load and can't do it myself," said Dad with a big smirk on his face, smiling at Mom.

"Okay you little angels, I would imagine you want to ride for a while. I need help in the cream room about three o'clock. Two or three of you will be enough for just doing the cheese curds. The driver will carry everything down to his truck with his dolly. There are chores to do this afternoon and biscuits to make as well as pudding and ice cream. Shall I leave all the decisions up to you as to how it will all be achieved? Our company should be here shortly after five o'clock," said Mom.

"We have it all covered," I said. "Thank you for lunch."

Everyone said thank you as we put the dishes into the dishwasher. Susie hurried and dragged Lorrel out the door to check out the tree house and rabbit home, as we sat on the porch and watched.

Before Lorrel could get dragged to the rabbits by his sister, he came back to the porch.

"Your tree house is a small cabin. You have the stairs wrapping around one of the cottonwood trees and a rope ladder, too. Your fire pole is so fun to slide down. I love all the windows. Your deck shows the whole country. I love the table and chairs and cabinets for crafts and games and walls full of puzzles and a chalkboard wall with coloured chalk. You forgot nothing. Wow, I want my parents to build me one like this. It is so funny shaped between these three trees. I did not realize just how fantastic this tree house is when we were designing ours at the church social." said Lorrel.

There is quite a story to the tree house. It has been over two years ago now, Jeff was having a terrible time figuring out a triangle project at school. He stood in the laundry room upstairs looking out the window and noticed the trees were in a kind of triangle. He figured out how to design a tree house and got honors for his off sided triangle blueprint design. He measured between the three trees, including the height with branches and he spent two days designing the shape and size. He had the doors and windows measured into it and when he brought it home, Mom and Dad figured they could make it reality. The next weekend Uncle Brian, Aunt Brenda, Mom and Dad built the tree house, with the help of us six kids. We sewed the curtains with Mom's help and made some rag rugs. Gwenie and Alan are making more rag rugs. We have been talking about painting it rainbow colours. "Jeff, did you really do up the blueprint for the tree house two years ago? It is fabulous," said Lorrel.

"It was real easy, once I understand the principle of triangles. Once I done all the measurements and my teacher checked on it, he offered some advice for windows with the direction of winds here. It was so much fun designing it and even more fun with the party we had here building it. Great Grandma and Great Grandpa figured I should go into drafting and work for them as soon as I am out of college," Jeff said as he laughed. "I am a farmer."

"Lorrel are you coming to see the rabbits?" Susie asked. "We are going to saddle our horses," said Jeff. "Later,"said Lorrel.

"My Dad says if we are going to keep riding and buy horses, he wants your Dad to build him the saddle system. It is beyond belief how great it works," said Lorrel, as we walked to the horse pasture and took our horses to the barn. In no time, the horses were saddled and we rode out of the barn.

"Is everyone comfortable in the saddle?" I asked, as we turned to ride down the driveway. We will do Grandma Linda's chickens and then we will ride her west land. We could never ask for a better no school day."

"I love riding. This is the greatest in the world. I love you are at the end of the road and you can ride anywhere," said Susie as she talked Ruby into speeding up a little. "When can we ride down that trail to the mountains?"

We dismounted at Grandma Linda's to do the chores.

"Okay, chickens and eggs are taken care of. Are you ready to mount up and explore the west country?" I asked. "That was cute Susie. I thought you were going to come right over and end up on the ground. Your parents would think twice about getting you a horse if you do a fall like that. You are just too funny." I said.

"I like to entertain. I will not fall. I might make you all laugh though," said Susie.

"Yes, she keeps us entertained all the time at home," said Lorrel.

We rode across the first quarter of land and into the second quarter. We rode down the draws and searched for animals.

"Ruby, gee. Gee Ruby." Susie said.

Whoa Ruby, Whoa. Back up, Back up Ruby," said Jeff. Susie, we do not go off the paths because of all the gophers and their holes. If a horse falls into one of their holes, they could be hurt. Now, if you look in front of you, you will see the ground is disturbed. That would be moles. They dig in the ground and tunnel all over. Sometime the mole tunnels are really deep. If Ruby falls through into one of their deep tunnels, you could fall off and Ruby could break a leg, which means she will be sent to horse heaven. We always have to watch carefully to make sure everyone stays safe. Now, Miss Leader, I want you to follow one of us until you understand all the dangers of riding in the wild," Jeff said, who was riding behind Susie.

"Okay, I am sorry. I did not know of all the extra hazards to riding. I love Ruby, I sure don't want her hurt," said Susie.

We have riden the full half section of land. We went up and down every coulee, gully, ravine, and valley. The sun was high in the sky and giving us her spring heat. The air was so fresh with a small breeze from the mountains. We were not sure who enjoyed the excursion more, us or our horses. We never saw the elk, deer or coyotes today.

"I guess we better be heading back," I said. "By the time we comb our horses, it will be time to help in the cream room. Jeff do you gentleman want to cook the ice cream mixture and make the ice cream? If you could cook four cups of rice for me, I will have time to do Great Grandma's recipe. After I mix up the cooked rice with ingredients, I bake it in the oven for ninety minutes. If you do that, we girls can help Mom and then we can come and help do chores. Our company is coming early. Does that work for everyone? I asked.

"Works for me," said Gwenie.

"Works for us," said Alan with a yes from everyone else.

"I love the way we can pick the saddles off our horses. We need this at home and some horses. Do you think we can buy Ruby?" Susie asked.

"No Susie that cannot happen. We have cousins who come and ride and we are short of horses if they all come in the summer at the same time. Beside, Ruby would miss all the other horses she was raised with," Jeff said.

We put the horses in the pasture and stood a minute to look at the perfectly blue sky. There was a shining silver blob high up leaving a trail of white behind it. None of us had ever been in a plane.

Gwenie and I went up the stairs to the cream room. We got suited up and went into the cream room. Mom was just bringing out the weigh scale so we could package the cheese curds. The boys plus Susie went to the house to cook the rice and ice cream mix.

"This is the last bag of cheese curds that we need for this order and I hear a truck. Maybe the driver is early," said Gwenie. "We have a couple of pounds of cheese curds left for us. I love cheese curds."

Before long the truck driver knocked on the door.

"Good afternoon Tim," Mom said.

"Good afternoon Breana. May I use your sink up here to wash these crates before I come in your cream room to fill them up? They gave me a different truck this morning and the last driver just didn't worry about dust or dirt, or grease. It is not a pretty sight," said Mr. Tim. "Good afternoon to you young ladies."

"Yes Tim, it is nice to see you again. I so appreciate the care you give. I had to phone your company and tell them never to send Lawrence here again," said Mom.

"Yes, this is his truck I have and I do not know if he still works for us today as he does get complaints because of his attitude," said Mr. Tim.

"Mom, I can take this cleaner and help Mr. Tim," I said. "Yes, please honey, and I will finish the book work here, and Gwenie will finish the packages for us," said Mom.

We washed the crates and in no time we had the crates full which Mr. Tim dollied to his truck. Mr. Tim washed his cup before he knocked on the door again.

"Thanks Tim, if you sign here, I will fill your cup with buttermilk and give you some cheese curds for your afternoon snack," Mom said.

"You spoil me," said Tim. "Thank you, I am off. See you next week," said Tim.

"Good bye Tim, Thank you for coming. Hope you can come every week," Mom said with a smile.

Mom walked downstairs with us. She opened the sliding door to let the milk cows come into the alleyway to the milking palour. We went to the house to prepare the rice pudding for the oven, before chores. Susie met us coming through the arch. She sat at the counter and watched us measure out everything that went in the rice to make the pudding. I put the pudding in the oven. The boys were just finishing cranking the ice cream maker. Such great ice cream. It is time for chores.

"I can surprise Mom with rice pudding and ice cream," said Susie.

"That is absolutely not possible, Susie. You are never to turn on the stove and start cooking without supervision, as anything can happen. You leave a pot holder to close to the fire and it starts to burn; you could burn down your house. That would not be a welcome surprise for your parents. You must be nine years old before you can turn on the stove and that is only after you have had years of helping and learning the techniques, right?" I said. "I believe you will have to learn some respect for the dangers that could happen before you get much older. You have away too much faith in plowing ahead with an attitude nothing bad could ever happen to you. Unfortunately, that is not how life works. We must always be on the outlook to recognize hidden dangers and prevent them from becoming reality and maybe a serious problem. Like today, with the mole holes. We prevented the chance of a serious accident to Ruby by stopping and rerouting her on safe ground. We must be on the watch always, to live a long, safe life, right?"

"I know all that, I am not a little kid, you know," said Susie with an attitude.

"Here is Dad with the last load," said Alan. "I am going to talk to Dad."

"Me too, I liked riding in the truck," Susie yelled as she ran to the mud room to put on her boots and ran out the door struggling to get her arms in the sleeve of her coat.

"Susie, Stop, Stop, Stop," Alan screamed, as Susie ran toward the truck.

The boys stopped putting the ice cream into the freezer container and ran to the window with Gwenie and I. Dad had just pulled ahead in the truck and was starting to back up to the auger. Susie was running to the truck. Alan caught up to Susie at the corner of the barn, and pulled her back. We opened the window to hear them yelling. Alan was really mad; scared Susie would have run behind the dual tires and got run over.

"You pulled me off my feet. I am telling my dad on you. You got me all dirty. What did you do that for?" whined Susie.

"Did you not hear me yelling at you? Did you not see Dad stop and start backing up the truck? We have rules here. Do you want to get run over? Your attitude is going to get you hurt."

"Hi Dad," Alan called.

"Hello. I am finished for the day, as soon as I am unloaded. Susie, what is the matter? What are you two yelling about?" Dad asked.

"Alan pulled me off my feet, and he hurt my bum," said Susie.

"Susie, tell the whole story, please," Alan said.

"How soon before my dad comes?" asked Susie.

"It depends if you are still alive by the time your dad comes because you have no respect for rules and your attitude is like a University Professor who thinks he knows everything and can do no wrong," Alan said.

"Wow that is pretty strong words. What did you do Susie? Dad asked.

"Nothing," said Susie.

"Dad, I am so glad you are home. I am helping Jeff and Lorrel make ice cream, so I am going back to the house and then we will start chores," said Alan. "Mom went to the cows about fifteen minutes ago."

We shut the window. The boys finished putting the ice cream in the container and were sharing the ice cream left on the beater. Alan walked in the door, as Gwenie and I were putting on our coats. He grinned at us and told us he was glad she wasn't his sister. We all laughed. It didn't take long with five of us doing the chores. Before we knew it we were back at the house. We washed our face and hands and walked into the kitchen.

"The rice pudding looks perfect," said Gwenie peering in the oven. "I will move out of the way so you boys can make biscuits. We girls have time for a shower before supper if you want," said Gwenie.

"Go and I will be right up behind you," I said.

When I came down the stairs, everything was set for supper.

"The McIntoshs are here and here come Mom and Dad up from the barn. That is perfect timing. The biscuits will be out of the oven in five minutes," said Jeff.

"Daddy, Alan is a bully. He pulled me off my feet and made me fall on my bum," said Susie to her Dad.

"Alan, what happened? Did you really do that?" asked Mom.

"Yes," said Alan.

"Whoa here," said Lorrel. "We were all in the kitchen when we heard Alan yell stop a few times so we opened the window. We heard and watched it all. Susie would you like to tell Mom what we seen?"

"You lie," said Susie.

"Lorrel, please tell us the truth," said Mr. McIntosh.

"Well, Dad, I will tell you the truth, which you will believe as there were three more pairs of eyes that observed it. Miss perfect would not listen to rules on riding the horse this afternoon and then when she seen Mr. McCarthy's truck come in the yard she was determined to get to the truck before it stopped and backed up. There are rules, here. If a vehicle is moving, we are not. We are standing safely away from danger and cannot go near any vehicle until it is stopped and we are acknowledged, or it is gone by. She was racing to the moving truck and would not listen to Alan yelling for her to stop until he grabbed the back of her coat and pulled her back on her bum. Alan kept her safe from being run over," Lorrel said.

"Susie, do you have something to say?" Mr. McIntosh asked.

"No," said Susie.

"Well, that is fine Susie. Let me apologize to every one for Susie's bad behavior. You are now grounded for two weeks. You will not leave the farm for any reason, as we will have a babysitter when we go to party. Don't give me them big dole eyes. If you had of been honest and apologized, this would have been forgiven with very little consequences but you made a mountain out of your bad behavior. Mom is this fair punishment for this bad behavior?" asked Mr. McIntosh to his wife.

"Absolutely. The McCarthy's are so overly good to us and you have to repay their kindness with your bad behavior. We are not impressed," said Mrs. McIntosh.

"I am sorry," said Susie.

"That apology is for nothing but your punishment, you will serve." said Mr. McIntosh.

"Thank you Heavenly Father for this beautiful day we have had. Thank you for all our friends, family, neighbours and loved ones. Bless us all Lord. Help us be your obedient children and help us to do your will. Bless this beautiful supper to our bodies use in Jesus name, we pray. Amen," Dad prayed.

"Supper was fantastic and the baked rice pudding with homemade ice cream is beyond words. I do not know how you manage," said Mrs. McIntosh.

"You have to thank the kids for supper," said Mom. "It takes a good seven hours to do cheese curds so the kids did the vegetables for the roast and they made the baked rice pudding and ice cream, as well as our grilled cheese sandwiches for lunch. I have some excellent little chefs here," said Mom smiling.

"Mom, I learned how to make grilled cheese sandwiches and homemade ice cream," said Lorrel.

"Excellent," said Mrs. McIntosh, "I believe I better add cooking lessons to your agenda."

"Thank you for just everything, for looking after the kids for us today and this excellent supper. We are the most spoiled neighbours. I have no idea how to repay you," said Mr. McIntosh. "We better get going as we have to do chores at Kopples before I do chores at home. Thank you so very much."

"You are so very welcome anytime. Thank you for coming," said Dad.

"Goodbye," was called by everyone, including Susie. "Mom and Dad, I love you. I would like to just go retire in my room now that the kitchen is cleaned up," I said.

"Us too," called everyone including Dad. "We will be up shortly to tuck you in bed, before we find our bed, early for once," said Dad.

15

Nap Land

"Good morning," Jeff called as he turned his alarm off.

"Good morning," was called back by our three sleepy voices.

It is Friday morning. We went to sleep. We woke up and ate. We went to school. We had snack and did the chores. We did homework and went to bed. The days just fell away. Tuesday, Wednesday, and Thursday we lived through. They were just normal days passing by.

"I am going to make fresh coffee for Mom and Dad, I said as I walked into the kitchen. "What do you want for breakfast?" I asked.

"Bacon, eggs and toast for me, thanks Jackie," Alan said. "I will get the toast.

"Sounds great," said Jeff. "I will do the bacon.

"I will set the table," said Gwenie, "Mom and Dad just walked out of the barn. We will be ready by the time they wash up."

"Hello," everyone called as they stepped through the arch. We all took our turns getting hugs, We all crawled on our stools at the counter and bowed our head as Dad said our morning breakfast prayer. He entertained us with stories of our milk cows that likes their singing. We enjoyed our breakfast with much laughter.

"I do not know how it got to be Friday already. You had Monday off and the rest of this week has just flown by with normal work. I am scared to blink my eyes if all the weeks are like this, you will be graduating from school before I can possible realize it," said Mom laughing.

"Let's do Bible study and then I will make your school lunch," said Mom.

"Our Bible devotion today is: *First Corinthians 10:31: Whatever you do, do it all for the glory of God.*

"With prayer from our happy heart we do our work the best we can focused on our Heavenly Father until we can join him in Heaven," said Jeff.

"Super, any more opinions?" Mom asked.

"Think that says everything," I said.

Mom made our lunches with our help. We brushed our teeth and put our coats on.

"Have a great day at school today," said Dad, as he was hugging us goodbye.

"We should be here for snack tonight when you get home from school," said Mom, hugging us.

We rode the bus to school, picking up our friends on

the way. Another day finished and we were happy to have the bus pull into our driveway.

"Thank you for the ride, Mrs. Jenkins. You have a great weekend. Can you cause something in town so we can skip school on Monday again," asked Jeff .

"Funny boy you are," said Mrs. Jenkins, "you all have a great weekend."

"Goodbye, and have a great weekend," we all called as we stepped off the bus.

Grandma Linda is here and we raced to the house.

"Hello" we all called as we bounded through the arch with clean hands and faces. We took turns hugging Grandma Linda, Mom and Dad. It is the greatest to come home and have snack with all the family.

"Tell us about your vacation," Gwenie said.

Let your dad bless our snack and I will tell you between bites and drinks," said Grandma Linda laughing.

"Heavenly Father, thank you for all the blessing you have bestowed on us this day, and thank you for bringing Grandma Linda home safely. Bless this snack to our bodies use in Jesus name we pray. Amen," prayed Dad.

"I got on the train and what a trip. The land is so beautiful. I left our beautiful trees to see different trees until I ran into palm trees. I will tell you, I will take our beautiful trees over those palm trees and hot, hot weather any day. Three days on the train and my sister picked me up at the train station in Lauderdale Florida. In a blink of an eye, she had me on a cruise ship, sailing the ocean blue. She was absolutely in her glory but I just wanted my feet on solid ground.

After five nights on that floating bath tub I was so glad to get back to my sisters condo. It is at the top of a very large building so you can see the whole city from up there. All night you heard vehicles, sirens, horns, air brakes, and people at that height. What you couldn't see was all the stars because of all the city lights. We traveled all over the country and ate at crazy little places. I have to tell you. My favorite thing was peanuts. They grow in the ground like potatoes. We can only buy roasted peanuts here. Well, there, they take those green peanuts, out of the ground and wash them and they put them in a big pot, bigger than our canning pot, full of boiling water and they boil them until they are cooked. They scoop them out, draining the water out of them and put them in a paper cup. They taste just like potatoes. No kidding, they are soft and hot and you peel the shell off and pop them in your mouth. They taste so much better than roasted.

We went to lots of parks and seen all kinds of sights. On one of our road trips, we were stopped for one hour and a half, waiting for an alligator to wake up and move off the middle of the road. They have the right of way, as if you try to move them, you could get their tail which would send you to never-never land. I had an excellent time with my sister and I cannot wait until she comes here to visit.

I will have her on horseback before she has her train legs sorted out. It will be a performance. She has not been here for over twenty years. She is city all the way, and loves the hot. I can just imagine her riding when the wind is blowing here a little," laughed Grandma Linda.

"It sounds like you had too much fun," said Alan, making everyone laugh.

" I am going to join you doing chores and I am invited for supper," said Grandma Linda. "I missed you all so very much."

"We missed you too," everyone said at the same time. Grandma Linda lives west to the end of old road and south, to the end of the quarter of land. She'd moved to the farm shortly after school when she married Grandpa Lorne. They had no children and Grandpa Lorne had an accident and passed shortly after Jeffrey was born. Grandma was a schoolmate of Grandpa Gary and Grandma Ella Katherine. I started calling them Grandma Linda and Grandpa Lorne, which tickled them pink and it became a permanent acknowledgment. Grandma Linda can do everything, as she worked beside Grandpa Lorne. She took over all the farm work after he was gone. She teaches us different things every opportunity she gets, with love and patience. We all learned how to crochet and knit, from her and Mom. She loves having our cousins come visiting so she can teach them, also. "It is so much more fun doing chores with you Grandma Linda and look how fast we got done," I said.

"More hands always means less work and it is fun to laugh and joke while we are working," said Grandma Linda. "I cannot wait to go see the Kopples home when they have open house. I am really looking forward to the party next Saturday."

Jeff parked the tractor and hooked up the hoses as Alan called to us to come to the pig barn. I just love it when new life is born. Soon we will have colts, calves, and lambs. Then our other Grandparents will be home with our dog who thinks it is better to go south with them in the winter than stay here and have us spoil her. It seems every animal on this farm can do exactly what it wants to do, when it wants to do it. Grandma Linda told us Chinook spent a lot of winters here on this farm protecting everyone. She can understand how she would sooner be in a warm climate for the winter. We walked into the pig barn.

"Oh they are such a healthy pink and beautiful. What great Mothers to birth such healthy piglets," said Grandma Linda.

"Let's head back to the house and set the table and then we can relax until your parents finish milking, okay?" Grandma Linda asked, as we walked away from combing our calves.

"Grandma Linda, you take the big easy chair in the living room and we will come join you as soon as the table is set," said Gwenie.

"Well, that was two minutes and Grandma Linda is sound asleep," said Alan, quietly. "Considering all the miles she put on, I can understand a long power nap. Let's go down stairs and get our homework done so that is out of our way for the weekend."

Twenty five minutes passed with us doing our homework. We saw Mom and Dad coming to the steps and waved them to the basement.

'Hello," we quietly called when Mom and Dad opened the patio door to the basement.

"Hello," Mom and Dad answered together, "where is Grandma Linda?'

"She is relaxing in the big chair in the living room and was sound asleep in two minutes so we thought we would let her rest, after her trip," Jeff said.

"Let us all watch the news and we can wake her up in half an hour, okay?" Dad asked. "Is your homework all finished?"

"Yes, we answered as we tucked our books away. It has been a long time since we just relaxed down here before supper," I said. "I like it."

"Me too," was answered by everyone.

"Hello," Grandma Linda called as she stood at the bottom of the stairs, seeing all of us stretched out in our recliners. We were staring at the television. There was a ship stuck in the ice somewhere near the North Pole. The news changed to the weather which they seemed to guess wrong about. Mom was the first out of her chair and walked to the television and turned the off button.

"We were just going to watch the news and come and wake you up, said Mom laughing. "Let's have supper."

We all climbed the stairs. Mom and I put supper on the table before we joined everyone else at the table.

"Heavenly Father, we thank you for this beautiful day. Bless us, Lord, and all our family, friends, neighbours and loved ones. Guide our bodies and mouth to do your will. Thank you Lord for this delicious supper we are about to partake in. Bless it to our bodies use, in Jesus name, Amen," prayed Dad.

"I just love being here with you all and thank you for this delicious supper. I am afraid that nap was just a temptation to find my bed, and now with my tummy full, I better bid you good night, before I fall asleep at the table. I will see you tomorrow, if you will excuse me without tea or dessert," said Grandma Linda.

"Absolutely, "said Mom, "We are so glad you are back home safe."

"A cup of tea might help you stay awake driving home or we could drive you home," said Alan. "Jackie made the tea already.

"Okay. You twisted my rubber arm," said Grandma Linda.

We enjoyed our dessert and the great company.

"When I drove in the yard, George and Raspberry tried to bring the fence down. I had to go pet them and triple locked the gate as Lucy was opening it when I reached it. They wanted me to spend the afternoon petting them when

I just wanted to visit with your Mom and Dad. I expect the coyotes to serenade me tonight, if I am awake enough to hear them," said Grandma Linda and she laughed and hugged us all good night."

We walked her to the door and then ran to the dining room and living room windows to wave good bye and watch her drive home safely. Mom and Dad stood beside us.

"Mom, all the dishes are in the dishwasher. May I be excused too please? I seem to be so tired after crawling out of the recliner," I said.

"Sure," Mom said as she moved to hug me, followed by Dad's big bear hug.

"Me too," my siblings called as they went for hugs.

Mom said thank you for all our hard work today as we walked up the stairs.

"We will be up shortly to tuck you in bed." Dad said.

16

RUSTLERS

'I heard the bluebird sing. It sang of waiting, waiting for the flowers' sang very loudly out of my clock radio before I could shut off the alarm. I was laughing when Jeff 's radio started singing the same tune, loudly, followed by Gwenie's, making us all laugh. Alan really knows how to start the day off .

We dressed and walked down the stairs to a serenade.

'sang of loving, loving every hour that I'm married, married to my flower. We'll be happy, happy ever after as since the day we've met. And though we're older, older the love is sweeter. We grow fonder, fonder of each other. We'll be sweethearts, sweethearts close together until the end of time,' sang Mom, Dad and Grandma Linda.

"Bravo, bravo, great singers." We said as we clapped our hands.

"Good morning." we said as we hugged and were hugged.

"Breakfast is ready." said Mom. "We were not fi fteen minutes behind you going upstairs and you were all sound asleep, already."

"I know the feeling. I did not even grab my suitcase out of the truck. I went inside, brushed my teeth and was in bed within fi ve minutes of walking in the house. If the coyotes serenaded me, I never heard them," said Grandma Linda.

"Heavenly Father, our Lord, thank you for this beautiful day you have given us. Bless us and keep us safe this day as we stride to do your will. Bless all our families, friends, neighbours and loved ones. Bless this food to our bodies use. We ask this in Jesus name, Amen," prayed Dad.

"What is the matter with George? He is making an awful fuss." asked Jeff "He wanted to get his two cents in during the blessing, eh?"

"Well, it is Saturday and he is anxious to go." Grandma Linda said.

"Go where? What's up? What are we doing?" asked Alan as we all waited for an answer.

"It's a surprise." Grandma Linda said. "Today, we are going to ride out and check the cattle. We have them all in the half section so I figure it will be a nice two hour outing. We will ride to the far end of the very north quarter. We will make sure we have them all and we will walk them all back through the gate to the south quarter and close that gate, keeping them here, close to the barn. We are locking them in a little early but it is such a beautiful day and they are talking about a snow storm next weekend. When I checked the calendar, I seen it was really foggy, for five days, ninety days ago Sunday, so I think we will have moisture. Rain I hope, but it could be snow." Dad said.

"Yes, yes, yes." We yelled as we were joined by the adults in our enthusiasm.

"Contagious, eh?" said Dad, which made everyone laugh.

Everyone chatted and smiled and laughed. Today we will all be where we want to be, in the saddle. Nothing in the world is better than riding. The world looks a whole bunch different from your saddle on your horse.

Breakfast was finished in record time and we rushed to put the dishes in the dishwasher. We nearly caused a traffic jam in the kitchen. Someone started to giggle which turned the entire kitchen into laughter. The race was on to be mounted in our saddle.

"If the ladies will clean up the kitchen, the rest of us can go do the chores." Dad said.

"Chores, what do you mean chores? On Saturday you always get the chores done. You are kidding us. It's nine o'clock. The chores are done." said Jeff, while we all stood like we were stuck to the floor staring at Dad.

Dad started to laugh, along with all the adults. "Yes, the chores are done. I was just seeing if you were paying attention. We will go saddle the horses, as we did not get that done this morning, yet," said Dad.

"The McIntosh's have just driven into the yard," I said.

"They are going to ride with us today," said Mom.

Everyone was laughing and talking as we put on our coats and boots.

"Welcome to this beautiful day of riding," Grandma Linda said to the McIntoshs, whom she had meet at many a give a helping hand function, and church.

"Hello, Linda. Welcome back to God's country. I hope you had a great vacation. Good Morning everyone," Mrs. McIntosh said.

We all welcomed The McIntosh family on our way to the barn.

All the horses wanted out of the pasture to roam free, so it took Dad a little more time to get the horses we needed.

"It was so much easier when only our horses were here." Dad said.

"Yes, when they all want to go, and we only need ten and George," said Jeff who was there super quick to help.

"George is determined to get his pack on first," said Dad.

Dad and Mr. McIntosh put the large packs on George. The pack is not that heavy but it is awkward for one person. Two pack boxes are joined by leather. When one person holds each box, they walk up each side of George and lay the leather over the blanket on his back with the joined box on each side. Front and rear cinches are tightened that keep it in place. The small packs are too small when packing lunch for all of us.

"George, go to the house." Dad said. "The ladies will take care of you."

"Lucy, you do not have to be saddled first. You are just too pushy." Dad said as Jeff was turning the tree to put Lucy's saddle at waist high as the men never used the hoist.

Dad took Lucy's halter off and put her bridle on. He straightened her saddle blanket and followed it with the saddle. After cinching it up, he tied the bridle reins on the horn and said "Lucy, go to the house."

"Okay Raspberry, you're next. Thank you for your help Mr. McIntosh. Are you comfortable grabbing the saddles, like this or would you like to use the hoist?"

"I am fine, thank you; it is a lot quicker to grab the saddles as compared to the hoist. We have a lot of anxious riders who want to be gone," said Mr. McIntosh.

"I promise you, every trip we do is with anxious riders wanting to be in the saddle and going," said Dad laughing.

"Thank you Jeff. You are such a big help." said Dad.

"No worries mate." Jeff said laughing.

As fast as the horses were saddled, the riders used the steps to mount and rode up to the house.

"Okay, we have Kernal, Lucy, Raspberry, Sapphire, Emerald, Topaz, Diamond, Opal, Amber and Onyx, and of course, George. We have them all so we can ride." Dad said.

George led the way down the driveway toward the road. In the bright sunshine, with a little west breeze blowing, we could not be happier with this life we loved and lived for. Turning west onto the road brought the mountains standing in all their glory, before us. The rocks were trying to peek through the layers of snow, covering them. The bright sunshine was showing off the layers of snow in the crevices and valleys.

"This is like heaven on earth. The air smells so good and the scenery is breathtaking, and having the privilege to ride an excellent horse that you can trust just makes the whole world a better place to live. It seems if we keep going west, we can follow that trail to the top of the mountains and ride off into the sky," said Mrs. McIntosh.

George turned on the approach that took us to the gate going into the north pasture. We followed and waited for Dad to open the gate. We rode through. George went toward the cabin as we turned to the northwest.

"George, you get over here. You wanted to come so you stay with us." said Grandma Linda.

We rode the first quarter and went through the open gate. We turned and rode along the fence line to the west. Once we reached the west fence line, we turned to the north, watching for the cattle. Being behind them makes it easy to push them east to the open gate.

"Dad, where are all the cattle? There wasn't any all the way west and we can see the fence line to the north and I still don't see any," I said.

"Well, honey, I don't know. They might be down in the coulee just over that little hill up ahead." said Dad.

"Dad, there is some on the other side of this fence. Look to the north by the trees." said Jeff.

"Well, we checked the fences just the other morning and made sure they were all in this half section." said Mom.

There were fresh tracks from a truck and the gate was opened. We had lost cattle to cattle rustlers for a few years. We were hoping we could get the cattle home before the rustlers showed up, this year. Dad asked us to ride west along the fence line and push the cattle back to the open gate as we searched to the north for them. He told us he would ride to Peterson's and call Sheriff.

"Dad, there is dust on the road. Look, it is a truck and horse trailer going down our private trail," said Jeff.

"Please round up the cattle. I am going to try and get them stopped," Dad said, as he clicked his tongue and Kernal took off like lightening. Kernal is a Rocky Mountain horse that stands sixteen hands high and he can run long distances fast.

Lucy who is a palomino standing just short of sixteen hands high wanted to join Kernal. Mom had to turn Lucy in a circle as she explained to her she couldn't join the stallion today. Kernal and Lucy normally were together on their excursions. We watched Dad jump the fence near the trail going to the road that went past the Peterson farm.

"I hate rustlers so bad. We take our new calves, when they are so young and burn their hides with our brand so we know they are our cows. Still people steal them. It is so very disgusting. I wish we could brand all the rustlers on the face so everyone knows they are rustlers and there every move can be watched," I said.

"These cows have been run with the truck by the looks of them. Is there a water hole open that we can walk them too?" said Mr. McIntosh.

"Just into the next coulee there is a deeper pond that we keep open and just checked two days ago. It should still be good but George, come with me and we will check if the water is open. If not, I have the axe in George's pack," said Mom.

"May I come with you and be your axe man if you so need?" asked Mr. McIntosh.

"Oh, how you remind me of my husband, Lorne. He was always the first to be a gentleman and help," said Grandma Linda.

"I cannot get over how beautiful this country is. Last week when I first climbed on Onyx, I thought I would die as I have never ridden before and now I believe it is my number one sport of all time. I cannot believe how great a person can feel riding the country horse back. This is heaven. Onyx just loves herding cattle too. This is too much fun," said Mrs. McIntosh.

"Where is your daughter today?" asked Grandma Linda

"She so misbehaved last Monday that she is grounded and has to stay on the farm for two solid weeks. There is a smaller home on our property and my Aunt Lilah moved in there, shortly after we moved here. She babysits Susie, and Lorrel, after school, and makes some of our meals. She is a godsent with us both working full time. We could not survive without her and she is so happy on the farm.

She has some sheep, chickens and turkeys today. I do not know what she might add tomorrow. You just have to meet her, she is just a treasure," said Mrs. McIntosh. "She is very involved with the church in town. She will come for the Kopple party.

"I am looking forward to meeting her," said Grandma Linda.

As Mom and Mr. McIntosh went to check the water hole, we rode to the west fence line and worked our way north. Lorrel and Alan turned down the first gully. Before long, we came to another gully that we could see our cattle down. Gwenie pointed out a trail running down. Grandma Linda and Mrs. McIntosh followed Gwenie down the gully. We kept riding until we came to the coulee. We could see to the far fence. There were no cattle up top so we dropped down following a cow path down to the bottom. We rode in silence until we rounded a curve and found at least sixty head. We both gave a sigh of relief, knowing we hadn't lost the whole herd. They were all milling around a flowing spring.

"Move em out! Head em up! Get along doggies!"
Jeff said that made us laugh. Sounded just like television.

We pushed the cows along the bottom of the coulee until it turned and the gully joined in. The ladies were walking behind about fifteen cows. There was no sign of Alan and Lorrel where their gully joined in. We herded the cows up the long sloop from the bottom of the coulee to where the trail went through the gate.

"Mrs. McIntosh, Onyx has been noted to bunt a cow on its rump if it doesn't want to move. I thought I should warn you. Onyx probably won't today as I told you but she loves doing it sometimes," I said.

"Hello, you ice choppers," called Mrs. McIntosh.

"Didn't take much," said Mr. McIntosh, "We will move our herd so yours can come water."

"There was a spring flowing down the draw, so our herd got to drink," said Gwenie.

"Ours too," I said so I guess we are good to the cabin. "Have you seen or heard from the boys yet and Dad?" I asked.

"Alan whistled a few times just a while ago and they waved when they went through the gate headed to the cabin, with all the cows from the east side of this quarter. Shall we move out?" asked Mom.

We walked the cows through the gate and across the land past the cabin. Lorrel and Alan were talking and watching the cows graze in the meadow. Grandma Linda told George to stay at the cabin as she and Mom rode ahead to the cow pasture in the farm yard. They undid the small gate going through an alleyway to the pasture so they could count the herd. We walked all the cows toward the opening and slowly pushed them until they all walked through the gate.

"I counted one hundred thirty-five ladies," said Grandma Linda.

"I got the same count, which means we are ten head short. I do not believe there could have been ten of our ladies jammed into that trailer when they are ready to calf in about three weeks. They either had another trailer or this isn't there first trip," said Mom.

"Oh, Mom, maybe Dad got to Peterson's in time to get Sheriff to catch them and we will have all of them back," I said.

"I hope so to," Mom said.

"I am going to close the gate and shall we go back to the cabin?" Mom asked.

"Raspberry, will you hold still. What did you do, grow three inches higher when I went to visit my sister?" Grandma Linda asked, laughing, as she lifted herself in the saddle.

"This cabin is so nice," said Mrs. McIntosh. "Thank you, Grandpa Lorne, that is Dad's Dad, build it when the family was real young as they came here to picnic and skate. The water is real shallow and spread out here so it was the best place for all their hockey games and pleasurable skating weekends. We added the calf shelter with benches inside it and you can see the nets and hockey equipment hanging on the back of the shelter. We had the equipment in the shelter but our cows were not happy until they dug it out and played with it. We would come to find it scattered all over the place. They even got the bag of hockey pucks open and I still do not think we found them all." Mom said laughing.

"Here come the boys with six more head. Dad is with them," yelled Gwenie excited.

"Great, that means we have only four missing. Hopefully Sheriff will catch them," said Mom.

"Mom, we boys will go put them in the barn yard pasture if you promise not to eat all the lunch," said Jeff laughing, as he joined Lorrel and Alan who were riding behind the six cows. They walked them to the gate and let them in to join the herd.

"I have Sheriff out searching for the truck and trailer and he has called in all his staff and the other close districts are watching too. They cut the chains at three of the closures we put up. The Peterson's did not see the truck and trailer go past to our pasture but they saw it come out. They did not recognize the truck. They did get a glimpse of the driver but didn't recognize him or the other two men in the cab," Dad said as he loosened the cinch on Kernals' saddle and hooked his bridle over the horn.

"Oh, I didn't tell you, we always loosen the cinch on the saddles and hook the bridle over the horn so our horses can move freely while we are resting. We trained our horses to stay fairly close and to come when we whistle," said Dad. "Otherwise it could be a long walk home."

"Excellent," said Mr. McIntosh as he loosened the cinch on Amber.

"Are you up for a long ride after lunch?" asked Dad.

"There is that gate on the Northwest of your land. It is about a four mile ride to there and we could ride your land and make sure you have all your cattle. We could lock them closer to your buildings until we are sure the danger is passed. This is the third year they got us. They come two weeks before calving. That is why we moved them closer to home, but not close enough, I see. They are determined rustlers. We better check Kopples on the way, and phone all the other neighbours and let them know. Is that too much riding for you today?" Dad asked.

"Sounds a perfect way to spend this beautiful day and maybe save some neighbours from rustlers and move my herd. I thank you for just everything you do for us. We can handle the ride, I am sure. Wouldn't it be nice to catch the rustlers," said Mr. McIntosh.

"Here come the boys. Let's eat so we can get on our way again soon. We can leave George at the farm. If he gets tired he will simple drift off into never-never land, some place. He will be safe at the farm with the other horses," said Grandma Linda.

"Okay boys, thank you for loosening your cinches. We are going to have a quick lunch and we are off on a mission. Can you handle another three hours riding today?" said Mom laughing, as the boys were pumping their fists in the air saying "yes" all at the same time.

"Heavenly Father, we thank you for this beautiful day you have given us. Thank you for the privilege of companionship in our walk on earth. Bless us and our neighbours,

friends, families and loved ones. Guide our tongues and feet to be of service to you Help us understand that there are bad things that happen on our walk of life and help us to deal with it without dishonouring your love. Bless this food to our bodies use. We ask this in the name of Jesus, Amen," prayed Dad.

"This is delicious; thank you," said Mrs. McIntosh.

"Thank you," was echoed by everyone.

"You are all very welcome. Dad, if you will bring George, we will pack him back up and let's tighten the cinches and be off," said Mom.

"I'll tighten your cinch Gwenie, being you grabbed the broom before I could get it," I said as I was laughing. I have to be fast to get the broom before Gwenie. She is always Miss Molly on the spot making sure everything is clean and tidy. No crumbs left anywhere to entice the rodents to come in for a snack.

We all enjoyed the ride back to the farm.

17

DESPERATE MEASURES

"George, come get your pack off ," said Dad. "Mom anything left in the cooler to put in fridge?"

"Not a thing. I will look after it when we get back," Mom called as Lucy turned to the driveway, again. "I believe Lucy understands everything we talk about, as she knows we are off again without George. Maybe she should learn to talk and she would pay for the whole farm, fast; A talking horse!"

"Can we ride ahead?" Jeff asked.

"Yes but be careful," called Dad.

"They are so far behind; we can herd Kopple's cows to the pasture by the house and catch up to them. I saw a gate to the east a little way up the pasture, when we were checking the cows," Lorrel said.

"Tight, this is so tight. I wish we had the gate opener with us. Got it," said Jeff. "I now need some help pushing the gate so I can lock it again. It is really tight."

"I got this," said Alan. "My lariat works great for tight gates."

"I am impressed. I never knew you knew how to do that. Great Grandpa showed me that trick years ago. I should carry a short rope. Better a short rope than your expensive lariat," said Jeff.

We all scanned the quarter of land for the cattle we could see near the fence line. There were some trees toward the south fence that would have to be checked. We girls rode down and checked for cows in the trees. We then pushed the herd back toward the gate meeting the boys who pushed the ones that were north of the gate. We closed that gate and the next cross fence gate, putting the cows in the pasture close to the barn. We rode to the gate and met the dog.

We all started to laugh when we checked the bull out. The bull was decorated with a piece of metal hanging off his horn. Broken red glass, a piece of rubber, a piece of white metal all mangled, was lying near the gate. This was not here when we were working here. The gate was barely closed. There was white paint on the side of the gate post.

"I think someone was in here this morning and the bull ran him out, and I am sure the dog helped. I can open the walk through gate easily on Emerald so we are leaving that way. I am definitely not getting down to open the other gate. I value all my body parts," said Jeff, making us laugh.

We rode down the driveway with the dog barking at us. We found a wrecked tire thrown in the ditch. It was close to the third power pole east of the pin cheery tree.

Sheriff Rasmussen will find it. We raced to the west side of McIntosh's land. Dad was just opening the gate. They all watched us race down the road to them. "Thanks, for keeping the gate open for us. We were too late for Kopples. The bull is wearing a piece of metal, He banged up a trailer, got the tail light and tire, which is in the ditch on the main road. The trailer hit the gate post on the way out leaving white paint. The dog is kind of woozy on its feet. They must have thrown it something to make it sleep or something, but the bull took care of them. We have no idea if they got any cows," said Jeff in a rush.

"Wow, we will call Sheriff as soon as we get these cows close to the house. No tracks here to be seen. We better call all our neighbours soon, too," said Dad.

"We saw some of our cows closer to the next quarter up in the corner there, so we will ride that way, and check the fences, as we go," said Lorrel.

"Thanks," called Mr. McIntosh to the back of us five riders as we were heading back to the corner to follow the fence line.

"Well, we got about forty cattle," said Lorrel.

"Forty-two, Lorrel, I counted them as they were strung out along the fence line." I said.

"Great, we only have thirty-three more to find," said Lorrel.

"The ladies are herding cows to the gate. We will ride ahead and see if we can count them," Gwenie said.

"Twenty-nine, I counted," said Gwenie. "Right, that leaves only four. Hopefully they are, oh, by the water trough. All seventy-five accounted for." I said. We rode behind the cattle pushing them through a gate and across more land toward the barn. We closed gates locking the cattle in the pasture. We went to a paddock beside the pasture and dismounted and undone our cinches. We followed the adults into the house.

"Lilah, this is Mrs. McCarthy, Mrs. Shields, Jacqueline and Gwendolyn," said Mrs. McIntosh.

"I am so pleased to meet you," Aunt Lilah said. "Lilah, can you help fix a snack and beverages for us please. We have to phone the police and then we will ride back to McCarthy's' place. We have cattle rustlers who we saw leaving the far north quarter of the McCarthy's place with four of their cows. It is so bad. We brought all our cows into the barnyard pasture. We will call all our neighbours too," said Mrs. McIntosh. "Where is Susie?"
"When Susie, saw you all riding in, she went to her room in tears. I sure hope she learns her lesson from this. When that girl gets a notion, she is gone and there is absolutely no stopping her, what so ever. When she gets in a mood, she will say that black is white and green is orange and get really indignant if you try and reason with her. She sure had her Dad buffaloed until there was witnesses to prove her disobedience. I am so glad he laid down her punishment and I pray he will stand behind it for the two weeks he gave her. If he gives in, we will never get a

handle on her bad attitude and actions. I love her to pieces and feel sorry for her but she has asked for this for years. Poor Lorrel has had a rough time at her manipulations to cause havoc and blame Lorrel for it, and deign the situation." Lilah said, as she was pulling warm cinnamon buns out of the bread keeper.

"What is this?" asked Mrs. McIntosh.

"Well, your children keep bragging about snacks, and desserts at the McCarthy's, so I decided I would give it ago. I used to make these when I was a child with my Mother so I thought I would try again. I made iced tea or we can do hot chocolate if everyone needs a warm up beverage after all that riding," said Aunt Lilah, smiling.

"Oh you are just too good to us, Lilah, we love you so much," said Mrs. McIntosh.

"You must come over and learn to ride. You will love it," said Grandma Linda.

"Absolutely, you must come over," said Mom.

We joined the boys and washed up. "Where shall we sit? I can't wait to have one of your cinnamon buns Miss Lilah," said Alan. "Oh, pardon me, I am Alan. This is my brother Jeffrey, my sisters Gwendolyn and Jacqueline." Alan said as he shook Miss Lilah's hand. Jeff shook her hand and told her it was a pleasure to meet her and called her Madam. Gwenie and I stood in the doorway, coming into the kitchen and watched Mrs. McIntosh, Mom and Grandma Linda exchange looks and smirk over the introduction.

"I am so happy to meet you. Our table has twelve chairs so please be seated at that end, so the adults can sit together at this end," said Aunt Lilah.

"Susie, would you like to come down for a cinnamon bun?" Mrs. McIntosh called up the stairs.

"I have to finish this first, I will be down later," Susie called.

"This is our Lilah. Best help in the world. This is Mr. McCarthy," Mr. McIntosh said.

"I am so very pleased to meet you Madam. Our door is always open to your company. Please feel free to phone and come visiting when you like," said Dad.

"Susie, are you coming down for prayer and snacks?" asked Mr. McIntosh.

"I will be down a little later," Susie called from upstairs. *"Heavenly Father, we thank you for this beautiful day and all the privileges you have bestowed on us,"* Mr. McIntosh was praying.

"Hello everyone," called Susie.

"Lord be with us this day and help us to do your work and guide us to help our neighbours with the trouble we have found," prayed Mr. McIntosh who was interrupted again.

"Hello, everyone, I will just sit here," said Susie.

"Bless *us Lord, each and every one of us and our families, friends, neighbours, and loved ones. Bless this snack to our bodies use in Jesus name we ask, Amen,"* prayed Mr. McIntosh.

"When do you think it is respectable to interrupt prayer?" Mr. McIntosh asked Susie with an absolute red embarrassed face.

"Well, Daddy, I missed you so very much I thought I would hurry down. May I share your saddle with you to take the horse back, Daddy? It would be so much fun. It would be just the two of us ridding one horse?" Susie asked.

"Who wants hot chocolate, or we have iced tea, hot tea or coffee if you please?" asked Aunt Lilah.

"Hot chocolate, please, "everyone at the table said. Mrs. McIntosh passed out twelve plates with a warm cinnamon bun on each. Aunt Lilah poured twelve cups of hot chocolate.

"These are delicious," said Grandma Linda, and we all agreed.

"Absolutely delicious Aunt Lilah, you are hired full time," said Mr. McIntosh laughing.

"I helped," said Susie.

Aunt Lilah started chocking on her hot chocolate and had to be patted on the back to stop the coughing. Mrs. McIntosh jumped up and got her a glass of water.

"How did you help, Susie?" asked Aunt Lilah.

"Why, I measured out the butter and put it in the pot to melt and I added the salt and four eggs, said Susie proudly.

"How did you add the eggs?" said Aunt Lilah. "That is all I did and I went to pick the eggs from the chickens," said Susie.

"I smell more to this story," said Mrs. McIntosh.

"Daddy, can we go ridding soon?" asked Susie.

"Why did you quit helping? How are you going to learn to make cinnamon buns if you quit helping?" asked Mrs. McIntosh.

"She didn't want my help anymore. She just wanted to tell you she done it all herself, I guess," said Susie.

"Susie, you tell the truth now, or I will," said Aunt Lilah.

"Susie, tell me the whole truth," said Mr. McIntosh.

"Oh, Daddy, these people are just trying to make trouble for us. This is so silly," said Susie.

"The truth now Susie," said Mr. McIntosh.

"Oh Daddy, the truth is I love you so much. Can we go ridding now?" asked Susie.

"Aunt Lilah, please tell me what happened," said Mr. McIntosh.

"Well, Susie thought it would be fantastic to make cinnamon buns just like the McCarthy's. Susie measured the butter and when it was melted she added the salt. We needed four eggs so she cracked the first one and watched the egg fall into the pot and threw in the shell. She cracked the next egg and threw it in the pot shell and all. I grabbed the carton of eggs when she would not stop. She managed to grab two more eggs and crack them and throw them in the pot, shells and all. She danced out of the kitchen, laughing," said Aunt Lilah, as I picked the shells out of the butter mixture. It is good we wash all the eggs or I would have had to throw it all out and start over again.

"Susie, what do you have to say?" asked Mr. McIntosh. "Oh, Daddy, everyone is just trying to make trouble for us," said Susie.

"Is that all you have to say?" asked Mr. McIntosh.

After we finished our hot chocolate and delicious cinnamon bun, Mr. McIntosh moved his chair to the centre of the kitchen, and sat down.

"Susie, come and sit on my knee," Mr. McIntosh said. "Oh Daddy," Susie called as she ran with her arm wide open.

Mr. McIntosh reached out and held her away from him. He looked in her eyes and said, "Where does my little girl come off with destructive behavior, interrupting prayer, and being the biggest liar I can't even imagine possible?"

"Now, I am going to give you something you have been begging for, for years. I want to let you know there is an endless supply of this. I hope just once will be all it takes to get you on the right path of life, of love and compassion as our Heavenly Father wants us to live. If once is not enough, I will do repeated lessons, on your bare bottom. Today, I will allow your bottom to be covered by your jeans," said Mr. McIntosh, as he lifted Susie over his knee and applied his bare hand to her bottom.

We all covered our ears as Susie screamed like she was being murdered.

"Have you learned your lesson with just four, Susie?" asked Mr. McIntosh after she quit screaming.

"I hate you," said Susie.

"Really?" said Mr. McIntosh. "Not I am sorry for the way I treat people and the way I act? Okay, four more this minute, should maybe straighten out that brain. We can do this all afternoon, but I would sooner go riding."

"If you keep screaming like you are being murdered, I will go get the belt so you will feel some pain. You know my hand is not hurting you that much. Now, do you have something to say?"

"You are just mean to me. I don't know why you are treating me this way. I am your little angel," said Susie.

"Lorrel, would you go up and get my belt off my suit pants, please. If that doesn't work, I will use my new fancy belt I got for Christmas. The beautiful tooled pattern will decorate her bottom," said Mr. McIntosh.

"Okay, okay, okay, I am not your perfect little angel when you are not here. I have raised trouble and lied about it. I was disobedient at the McCarthy's. I have tried to get Lorrel in trouble all the time because he just does everything he is told and he is always your great help. If you forgive me, I promise to be better. If you give me another chance, I promise not to try to be the boss and make my own rules. I promise not to disrespect you any more Aunt Lilah. You know how bad I have been so many times. If you can forgive me I promise I will try and be your better niece. If you will all please forgive me, I will try really hard to be a better person," said Susie.

"Who else do you need to ask for forgiveness and ask to help you be a better person?" asked Mr. McIntosh.

"Okay, Heavenly Father, please forgive me for all the bad little things I did. You know there are hundreds of problems I tried to cause, along with all the ones I caused and hid the truth. Please help me to be truthful and honest and helpful. Oh, please forgive me for the person I was and try to make me be the person you want me to be.

Lord, you promise you will forgive me if I ask. I ask and I ask if you will help my family and the McCarthy's to forgive me to. I don't want to be me anymore. Amen." Susie said with tears flowing down her cheeks like a waterfall.

"Okay, let us start a fresh calendar," said Mr. McIntosh. "You know you have all of our love, but you will have to earn our trust by being obedient, right?"

"Yes, Dad, I am going to try my best to be good and not naughty. I am sorry I threw the egg shells in with the cinnamon buns. I knew better but done it to be mean. I am so sorry Aunt Lilah. You made beautiful buns, in spite of me. Mom, I will get your jewelry that I hid on you. I am so sorry. Lorrel, I will get all your homework I hid on you. I am so sorry," said Susie.

"Thank you, Susie for all the truths revealed. We will all pray for you, as well. You know we all love you," said Mrs. McIntosh.

18

Back in the Saddle again

"Let's call a few more of the neighbours and get them to spread the word and we better get back or we will be doing chores in the dark," said Mr. McIntosh grabbing the phone.

"Oh, the police should be at the Kopples soon. "Thank you for snacks Aunt Lilah," we all said as we cleared the table of all the dishes and cups. The adults were still sitting at the table with the telephone.

"We look forward to having you over to ride with us, soon," I said as we walked out of the kitchen.

We had permission to ride. We went to our horses and tightened the cinch. Lorrel led Opal to the clothes line platform and stepped into his saddle. We smiled as we climbed into our saddles. We rode out the driveway and down the road to home.

"I sure hope life will be so much better with Susie. I like her when she isn't trying to be bad. Lorrel, she must have stolen a lot of homework for you as you were locked up for a lot of lunch time detentions," said Jeff.

"Thirty times, plus poor grades and Mom and Dad would not believe I done my homework. I got so I would show my work to Aunt Lilah so she knew I done it. Oh, I am so glad that is all behind me. She can be a good sister. I do love her. I just didn't love what she done to be naughty," said Lorrel. "I have never been spanked in my life. If Mom or Dad told me something, I did it, although Susie tried to get me spanked."

"I love this country. It is beyond beautiful. What a day for a ride. Let's get some speed going," said Lorrel. "We got chores to do. I love helping at your farm because everything is set up so easy to get the work done with no effort and fast."

"Here comes the sheriff. Let's stop at the tire," I said.

"Howdy," said the sheriff, "A beautiful day for a ride."

"Howdy," we all said.

"In the ditch here is a tire that looks like it was torn apart by a bull. It even has a rim on it," I said. The trailer was in the Kopple's pasture, where the bull beat the trailer up. The bull is still wearing some metal. There is metal and red glass from the tail light. There is white paint on the gate post where the trailer rubbed. The dog had been drugged or something, as he was really foggy when we were there. We don't know if he stole any cows here but he got four of ours. We saw him leaving the pasture, down the old trail when we were riding there this morning," I said. "I think the truck is a dirty reddish color. Did you catch him yet?"

"We are working on it. Thank you for all your information," You all have a great ride and a great afternoon," said the sheriff.

"Thanks, goodbye," we all said as we rode away.

"I would have warned him about the dog but he knows it all," said Jeff laughing.

"He will find out for himself. He did not seem to appreciate our information," said Alan.

"Let's speed it up for a while and then we can walk them closer to home so they are cooled off, okay?" Lorrel asked.

"I love this beautiful weather. Aunt Lilah sure does know how to make cinnamon buns. What a snack. They were excellent," Gwenie said.

"Yes, that was the first time and how great. Perfect timing to make them when we could all share them," said Lorrel. I will run the hoist, if you don't mind,"

"We had that figured out. We all know how we have to figure out a new machine and make sure we know exactly how it works," said Alan laughing. "You know exactly how to shift the big truck, right?"

"Absolutely," said Lorrel with a big grin of his face. We rode down the roads in the beautiful sunshine. A plane flew over shining in the sun and leaving a trail behind. A deer jumped the fence and left for greener pastures, away from horses and riders. Too soon we were riding into the barn. We undone our cinches and the boys removed our saddles. We combed our horses in the sunshine in front of the barn.

"Okay girls, you got your treats, and you have been combed. Come back to your pasture. Come, now," I said. "These treats are for your sisters that had to stay home."

Gwenie told me she had everything we need for the chicks and turkeys when we met on the way to the old barn.

"The boys must be cleaning the pens in the pig barn. I heard the little tractor start," said Gwenie.

"We could just about use the tractor in here. I do not know how they could make this waste, so fast," I said laughing. "I am bringing the wheelbarrow."

"Finished, at last," said Gwenie.

"Let's go get their clean bedding before we do the laying hens and milk cow pens, okay?" Gwenie asked.

"A change of chores for a minute will be a great relief, for sure," I said.

We threw down wedges of hay and straw into the aisle below. We gave the chicks and turkeys clean straw and hay. We collected the eggs and cleaned the floor for the laying hens. We filled their feeders with feed or water and then spread new hay and straw on their floor. The cow pen was mostly clean. The water hose made short order of washing the waste down to the sludge pit. We walked to the new barn and were nearly finished with the eggs when Jeff came up to see how much more time we needed.

"The barn looks nice, girls, are you nearly ready to do the calves," asked Jeff.

"We are on our last carton, before we put them in the cooler," called Gwenie.

We walked to the calf pasture, together.

"All our calves sure have been spoiled tonight with you helping comb them too Lorrel," said Jeff. "Let's go watch television, With all the excitement today, I could use a few minutes in the recliner chair."

We walked to the house and settled into our recliners with Walt Disney Bambi on the television. "Are you hungry?" Dad asked, from the stairway.

"Yes," I said, waking up. "Lorrel is gone. We never even said goodbye. News was on the television."

"I sneaked in an hour ago and quietly woke Lorrel up so he could go home with his parents. We just finished milking. Come on up for supper, now." Dad said as we laughed.

"Did the sheriff get eaten by the Kopple's dog? He was so nasty, we did not warn him." I said.

"You are right about him being nasty. They gave him a promotion so he is rude with it. Come Monday, I will have all the answers from our friend Sheriff Rasmussen," said Dad.

"Dad, can we say an extra prayer for Susie, tonight? I think she is a good kid that just started down the wrong path and she learned a big lesson today. She had to learn the hard way as two weeks grounded meant nothing to her," I asked.

"Heavenly Father, thank you for this beautiful day we enjoyed. Lord I pray that the rustlers have had a scare enough today that they will quit stealing from farmers. Lord, we ask that you touch Susie's heart and help her be your obedient child. Bless us and all our neighbours, family friends and loved ones. Guide us to do your will. Bless this food to our bodies use. We ask this is Jesus name, Amen." Dad prayed.

"Grandma Linda made us supper tonight while Dad and I did the milking," said Mom.

"Oh thank you Grandma Linda. It is a good thing you didn't come down to help us watch television or you would have been found with us," I laughed.

There were fifty-two good recliners in that turned over truck and trailer Dad purchased from the insurance company. There was only three that were really messed up and they redid them at McCarthy Lumber and Construction. They put calf hides on the back so they had enough leather to fix the rest of the chairs. We should have taken a picture of them. They were just beautiful. There seems to be a flaw in all the recliners. Mr. and Mrs. Webster said they are so glad they put the chairs in their home and not in the office at their western wear store. Mrs. Webster says she has to make supper before she sits a minute or it is too late, when she wakes from her nap. Dad told us we have six recliners that cost the price of just one if we had of went to the store to purchase it.

"Supper is great. Thank you. Does anyone want dessert?" asked Mom smiling.

"Yes, please," we all said, echoing Dad's words that were spoken first.

"Are you up for a game, tonight," Grandma Linda?

"I am sorry. Tonight my recliner is calling me very loudly. It was such a beautiful day of riding around the country. A very strange day it was with the rustlers and Susie's performance. I believe I better go home and my recliner will help me make sense of this crazy day," said Grandma Linda smiling.

We finished dessert and cleaned the table and kitchen, while the adult enjoyed a cup of tea. Grandma Linda stood up and said she had to go before she was too sleepy to drive. Good night and I love you was spoken by all with hugs. Mom asked if we were up for games tonight. Mom laughed when we told her our beds were calling us and Dad said his bed was definitely calling him.

"Thank you," said Mom as we took the cups off the table to the dishwasher. "My bathtub and bed are calling me. I will be up shortly to tuck you in."

Dad grabbed Mom and was hugging her when we climbed the stairs.

19

MORE BRANDS

'I'm looking over a four leaf clover I overlooked before. One leaf is sunshine the second is rain. Third is the roses that grow in the lane:' loudly sang from Jeff 's radio.

Gwenie's radio, then my radio erupted in song as Alan laughed in his bed.

"I have no idea where you find the time to program these songs for our alarm clocks." I said.

"That is my surprise to you and a good morning. Now you will be humming that tune all day," Alan said laughing.

We dressed and met in the mudroom. "Flashlights, okay, let's go get our chores down." Jeff said.

Jeff parked the tractor and turned it off at the chick barn. "Jackie, Gwenie, come out here please. Listen to the morning," said Jeff .

"Our cows are mooing in our pasture here and it sounds like there are cows west of Grandma Linda's place. What is up with that? Grandma Linda sold all her cattle," I said.

"Thank you for confirming what we thought we heard," said Jeff. "We will help you as soon as we put the tractor away."

"Our calves are restless this morning. They do not like whatever they are hearing from over southwest," I said.

"Okay, I think we are ready for showers and our church clothes," Gwenie said.

"Dad, Mom did you hear the morning? Did you hear anything strange from around? You can really hear the morning from in front of the pig barn but you can hear it here if you listen closely, I think," said Jeff.

"Is this that important?" asked Mom.

"Absolutely; it will only take a moment. Let's go stand in front of the house, okay?" Jeff asked.

"Our cows are restless and calling and their call is being answered by cows southwest of Grandma Linda's where there are no cattle," said Mom.

"Right, I knew you had to hear this. They just started it about fifteen minutes ago when dawn was breaking. Maybe our four cows are there, calling for their friends locked up here," I said.

"Can we saddle up and ride over there now?" I asked.

"I want to go so bad now, but the proper thing to do, in our Lord's eyes, is to go to his house of worship and pray, the cows will still be there after worship," said Dad.

"Showers, and good clothes, breakfast and church is on our schedule at this moment," said Dad.

"Heavenly Father, we thank you for this day of worship. Lord, you know our hearts and our love for you. Lord, as you know, we believe we might have heard our stolen cows this morning. Please protect them until we can check them out after we have the privilege of worshiping you in your house. Bless us Lord and all our friends, families, neighbours and loved ones. Thank you for all the blessing you bestow on us. Bless this food to our bodies use. In Jesus name we pray, amen," said Dad.

"Thank you for breakfast. Do we have time to prepare lunch, now so we can ride sooner?" I asked.

"Honey, grab the crock pot. I am going to get some packages out of our freezer. We will have this all done before we brush our teeth and be in the van. Here comes Grandma Linda. I do not know why she did not come for breakfast," said Mom.

"Did you listen to the morning?" asked Grandma Linda.

"Yes, we have lunch on the go in the crockpot so we can eat and ride," said Mom.

"I made some phone calls to have the trail watched until we can deal with it," said Grandma Linda.

"All aboard," Dad called as he climbed into the driver's seat.

We rode quietly in the van to church. We greeted everyone and went to our Sunday school classes. We sang the songs during the Church service. We hurried to the van when it was finished.

"That is the longest church service I have ever heard," said Grandma Linda.

Dad who was laughing said, "We are even out today ten minutes early. I told the folks that wanted to visit we had a situation at home. Let's go fix it. Okay, my little angels, what is your Bible verse today?"

We each looked at the other in total silence, trying to remember what it was, as the adults shook with trying to quietly hold their laughter in.

"Well, it was nothing about rescuing our cows," said Gwenie laughing, followed by the roar of laughter in the entire van.

"In all the years of us going to our church and having to mesmerize a special Bible verse, this is the first time you cannot remember it. Do you remember what your Bible lesson was about?" asked Mom.

Alan started to laugh again which got the whole van laughing again.

"Mom, Grandma Linda, do you remember what the service was about?" asked Dad.

After a long minute of silence, everyone was laughing again.

"Oh, my eyes are leaking," said Gwenie, which was hardly understood with her laughter.

This is what they call distracted attention. We all went to our lessons; participated in the class; sang during the church service and cannot remember what we learned. All we know is we think we heard our stolen cows.

"Well, we will not forget lunch," said Dad laughing.

It took forever for us to get home. Grandma Linda took clothes out of her locker and went into the bathroom as we ran up the stairs with our barn clothes.

"That did not take three minutes for you to run up the stairs and come down in your barn clothes. Are you in a little bit of a hurry?" asked Dad laughing as Grandma Linda walked into the arch in her barn clothes after changing in the bathroom in the mud room.

"Heavenly Father, we thank you for this day. Help us and guide us and all the others involved to be safe in our afternoon travels. Bless this food to our bodies use. We ask this in Jesus name, Amen. Dad prayed.

"This is delicious. Thank you," said Jeff .

"It is absolute delicious, thank you," we echoed.

"Are we all ready for dessert now?" Mom asked.

"Can we save it for snack if that is okay?" I asked.

"We will clean the kitchen if you want to get changed and we will be saddling our horses, okay?" said Jeff,

"I guess there is no lingering over a cup of tea," said Grandma Linda laughing, heading for the mud room.

"Wish we were strong like Dad. We could throw the saddles on instead of using the hoist. Lucy, go to the house, Kernal, step right up. They love going for rides, George is making more noise and braying like we are hurting him. Leave him behind and he sounds like Susie.

Mr. McIntosh hardly made a sound, giving her a spank and she screamed like she was being burned alive. I know it hurt him worse than her. I pray all that bad behavior is behind her. She is one very smart young lady. She just asked for a spanking. She refused to be honest until she got it, twice, in front of all of us. We have all been smart enough to never have had a spanking. Okay Kernal, go to the house. Raspberry step forward." Jeff said as Alan worked the hoist and saddle tree.

"We might have to take George or he might bring the whole farm down. Our cows were upset this morning; I can't imagine how they will feel with hours of George screeching like that. And, you are right. Susie, five in eight months is one smart young girl. I pray she got it figured out and will be positively honest and truthful," said Alan as he lowered the saddle on Emerald.

"Hi Dad, we are getting them saddled," Alan said.

"Perfect, and I think we better take George with us," said Dad.

We had the horses saddled and we all mounted and headed down the driveway.

We are not going to race. It could be a very long ride again this afternoon. After having them out most of yesterday, we must ride them easy, today to not tire them out. As much as they would love to run, we must protect them. They will all be new mothers in a month.

"We have another perfect day of riding with the mountains standing there in all their glory watching over us.

Your Grandpa Lorne and I use to go riding at least five times a week when it was so beautiful like this," Grandma Linda said.

"I am so sorry he got called home so young. Wouldn't he have enjoyed this day," said Mom.

"Yes, I miss him every minute," said Grandma Linda. "We can leave this gate open and standing up along the fence, in case we get a whole herd of cattle. We don't need them standing on it. This is hard to believe. I hope our ladies are here among whatever we are going to find," Dad said.

"Dad, I have butterflies in my stomach," said Gwenie.

"I believe we all have some butterflies,"Mom said.

"Dad, shall we leave this gate open, too?" asked Jeff as we had crossed the first quarter of land.

"I think so. It will be easy to keep them moving through here right to Grandma Linda's corrals."

"Dad, shall we split up. We could ride the north fence line down to the west and ride along the west, pushing all we find to the east. There is a coulee and draw before half the quarter, so we could work at least half," Alan said.

"That sounds good. We will ride up on top here to the south as we can see most of the land, other than the coulee to the south fence where I know there is a gate, and an old wagon trail," said Grandma Linda. "Bye, be safe."
"Be safe," Mom and Dad both called, 'Love you."

"Love you too," we all called together as we were riding to the west.

"There are ten down that draw that I can see. Who is going down?" Alan asked.

"If you boys want to do this draw, we will ride to the coulee," I said.

"Meet you in the middle, Gwenie said as we rode to the south.

"There are our four cows. See the brand? Oh, and them five. One of our 4-H members has that brand. There are four more here around the bend. Those rustlers were busy but we got them this year. I hope we have every cow they rustled so they have nothing to show for their devils work," I said "Here the boys come with fourteen cows, I think. "They were busy rustlers."

"Up, up you go. That path is not too steep. Get along, now," Jeff said as we herded the cows out of the coulee. Here, comes Mom and Dad and Grandma Linda with seven cows.

What a great day, and a beautiful ride. What an honour to find our cows and our neighbours cows. Most won't even know they are lost yet. This day has brought us such blessings.

We slowly rode herding the cows through the gate of the west quarter. We kept them walking through the east quarter. We walked them through that gate, across the road and on the way into Grandma Linda's corral. Dad shut the gate to the land, as our four cows hurried out of Grandma Linda's yard and started heading down the road to home. Sherriff Rasmussen, who was parked in Grandma Linda's driveway, shut the gate to the corral, to keep the other cows in. He was the one who helped with the rustlers last year, although they couldn't catch them.

"Grandma Linda, do you have the area brand book?" asked Dad.

"I have an old one from when I owned cattle," said Grandma Linda. "I am sure Sheriff has one. He is right on the ball. I cannot imagine how they hired that other can't listen, know it all. Maybe he needs turned over someone's knee," Grandma Linda said that made us all laugh.

"Good morning. I see you brought us some cows. That is excellent work. Maybe, I should deputize you all," said Sheriff Rasmussen smiling, as we rode out of the yard following our cows down the road, with George leading the way. If they could open the gate themselves at home, we would not even have to go. I opened the gate and they walked in together. Some of the herd was milling around close to the gate and immediately went to rub up against them when they walked in. They must have had quite the experience yesterday being chased by the truck and captured. We hope Sheriff can catch them. We turned our horses to Grandma Linda's, after we put George in his pasture. He was taking no chance of being anywhere but here. In minutes we were putting our horses in the corral at Grandma Linda's.

"Diamond, please stand still so I can loosen your cinch," Gwenie said laughing.

"I can smell warm spice cake and I bet Grandma Linda is putting that brown sugar icing on it that she cooks. I have to learn how to do that. It is so delicious,"I said.

"Hello, we smelled your cake from the gateway. You spoil us and we love it," said Alan.

"Come and have a chair. It will be out of the oven in ten minutes," said Grandma Linda.

"Heavenly Father, we thank you for this beautiful day you have given us. We thank you that we could rescue our cows and the neighbours cows from the rustlers. Bless us, Lord and all our families, friends, neighbours, and loved ones. Guide us to do your work. Bless this snack to our bodies use. We ask this is Jesus name, Amen," prayed Dad.

"We have seven farmers on their way here as soon as they hook up their trailers. They had no idea that their cows have been rustled. The trailer, which they left with the cows, was stolen two years ago, about one hundred miles from here. The insurance paid out, well, paid out what little they figured. I can never figure how you pay top dollar and if something happens, it's not worth much. Some things in life we have to live with and Insurance must be one," said Sheriff Rasmussen. "But on a positive note, life is so much easier when we have these brand books to identify the owners.

"That is the honest truth," said Grandma Linda.

"Do you have more or less work to do now that you have that new Officer?" Mom asked.

"I have to deal with a whole bunch more people. He does not seem to have any respect for folks at all. He graduated from the academy so that makes him a big hero in his way of thinking and everyone is beneath him. He will not listen to anyone. He jumps to concussions and then tries to prove what he thinks. I sent him off to a special class for a week to learn about evidence but I just wasted money. A letter came after the class asking me never to send him on anything again. They called him an arrogant know-it-all, who could do nothing but disrupt classes. I am trying to get rid of him. It is much harder than you think. I think I hear the first unit driving in. Thank you for the beautiful snack as you call it. Your cake is fantastic," said Sheriff Rasmussen.

We quickly put the dishes in the dishwasher and hurried out to the pasture.

"Hey Jeff, are you stealing our cows now?" Butch called from the truck door.

"You should thank me," said Jeff. "Rustlers stole four of our cows yesterday off our northwest half section. We heard them this morning a half mile to the west here. We found thirty-four including our four cows. They left the trailer behind that they have been using to rustle with. We checked Kopples and the bull tore up the trailer some and wrecked a tire. He hit the fence post on the way out. He didn't score at Kopples. I think there was too much traffic so he didn't steal any from McIntoshs either. He rustles in the day, so I guess he figured he would be safe stealing from you, undetected." Jeff said.

"Wow, we lost five last year too. Just about this time of year, before calving. I guess they haven't caught the rustlers yet?" said Butch. "Oh, we are ready to load. Are you coming to help? That didn't take much. It was like they smelled our farm in the trailer and they want to go home," Butch laughed.

"Yes, our cows nearly ran down the road to get home," Jeff said.

"See you on the bus tomorrow," called Butch, as his Dad pulled out and another truck and trailer pulled in, with Tom and his Dad.

"Alan be careful! That cow is so happy to smell that trailer he is kicking for joy. I sure don't want to see you kicked," said Jeff.

These cows smell their trailers from down the road and they line up to get into them and back home I think. Strange, but being rustled is strange, I guess. More trucks and trailers were coming down the road.

"Jeff, how do you have our cows?" Tom asked as he got out of the truck.

Jeff repeated the story and was rewarded with praise.

"Great work. We lost five last year. Glad we got these back. Oh they nearly ran into the trailer. Bye," said Tom, getting in the truck as his Dad got into the driver's side.

"Bye, see you on the bus tomorrow," said Jeff.

Only one more trailer was left to come. There was enough help here, so we were not needed. We got our horses and tightened the cinch. We led them to the step where we stepped into the saddle. We rode home feeling like heroes.

"What a successful day. We got one up on the rustlers, this year I hope. I just wish they could catch them. It would be nice to put a stop to this. We should enjoy our rides and not worry about finding rustlers," I said.

"That truck and trailer is pulling in our yard. I don't know those folks. Let us hope it is the folks for the last five cows and not the rustlers," Gwenie said.

"Howdy," said the driver. Do you have some cows here that do not belong to you?"

"No sir," said Jeff , "If you go to the end of the road here, and turn south, you can pull in the yard and back up to the chute. Sheriff Rasmussen is waiting there for you. You have the last five of thirty-four we rescued this morning," said Jeff .

"Thank you so much," the driver said as he started pulling around to head out the driveway.

What an inconsiderate driver. He could not wait a minute for Emerald and Jeff to get well away from his truck and trailer. He has no rules. Emerald and Jeff were fine but they would sooner be more than two feet away from a moving vehicle. We are just spoiled with our safety rules, which we love. I wish everyone would have the same safety rules.

We rode into the barn. The boys took our saddles off first. The only time us girls can run the hoist is if the boys are not with us. They are such gentleman they think. We like running the hoist. We brought our horse out in the sunshine and combed them for twenty minutes. We gave treats to the horses left in the pasture when we took our horses back to their pasture.

Together we walked to the feed shed and started on our chores. The cattle were all very content in their pasture. They were all together with bales of hay and a trough full of water, and a mineral block. The sheep were no longer restless because of the upset cattle. They had most of their mineral blocks left, as well as bales of hay. The sows were happy to get into the sunshine and enjoy their supper. It seemed the chicks, turkeys and laying hens had not been disturbed by the morning cattle calls. In short order we had the chores done and walked back to the barn together. Mom, Dad and Grandma Linda were riding up the driveway.

"We will take your saddles off and comb your horses if you want to start milking," I said.

"Thank you. We are going to take you up on that generous offer. The faster we are finished, the more family time this evening." Mom said.

Grandma Linda went and got George to comb as we combed Raspberry, Lucy and Kernal. Raspberry is a palomino standing fifteen hands high. George was so happy to be combed; he threw his head up in the air and brayed.

We all laughed. We locked them in the pasture, after Lucy led them back into the barn for treats and walked to the house together. It didn't take long to get our boots off. "I am so glad chores are done. It seemed to take forever tonight. What are we going to make for supper?" asked Jeff.

"We are having spice cake for dessert," said Grandma Linda. "If I keep it at home, I will eat it all and Raspberry will not like my extra weight on her back."

We have elk sausage." I said as I searched in the deep freeze. "We haven't had elk sausage for a long time so how about it with scrambled eggs and hot cakes?"

"That sounds perfect for me," said Grandma Linda. "Grandpa Lorne loved his hunting and he shot an elk every year. It is just the best meat."

"Someday, Mom promises, we are going to have a very relaxing Sunday afternoon and maybe play some of our games," I said. "I just wonder if it will be this year. We seem to just keep so very busy," I said laughing.

20

THE GLASS

I put the frozen sausages in a pot of hot water and put them on the stove to defrost and cook. We pulled the dice game out and Grandma Linda wrote our names down on the score pad. Grandma Linda started the game by dropping all five dice. All five dice had four up. Nice way to start we all said, as we took turns shaking the dice.

After twenty minutes we got up to go to the kitchen. Grandma Linda sliced the sausages. Gwenie cracked the eggs in a bowl as Jeff and Alan mixed up the pancake batter. We got the sausage browning in the fry pan. Gwenie got the eggs whipped with cream and dumped them into the hot fry pan. Jeff was making hot cakes. Gwenie and Alan set the table as I reached the glasses. Everything we needed was on the table when I filled the glasses with buttermilk.

"Supper looks great," Mom and Dad said together, making us all laugh.

"You owe me a coke!" said Mom and Dad.

"You still play that game?" asked Grandma Linda. "Grandpa Lorne and I use to say that when we said the same thing at the same time. Great minds think alike, folks say."

"*Heavenly Father, we thank you for this beautiful day. We thank you that all the cows are returned to where they belong. We thank you for all the blessing and privileges. Bless us and our families, friends, neighbours, and loved ones. Bless this food to our bodies use. We ask this in Jesus name, Amen,*" prayed Dad. "This is so delicious. How did you know this is exactly what we wanted for Sunday supper?" Dad asked smiling.

"Good guess," said Alan smiling, which got us all laughing.

"Do you want cake?" I asked. "I am going to save mine till snack time after school tomorrow."

"Just tea, please, for me," said Grandma Linda. "Supper was perfect, thank you."

I helped my sibling bring all the dirty dishes to the dishwasher. The tea kettle started to boil as we had the table cleared and the kitchen cleaned up. I made the tea and put it under the tea cozy on the table as Gwenie put the cups on the table. This is Sunday night. The day full of surprises is coming to an end and I am ready for my bed.

If you will excuse me, I am going to get ready for bed." I said. "It seems to have been a long day."

"Me too," was echoed by my three siblings.

"I love you," said Grandma Linda as she stood up from the table and hugged us all.

"Love you too," we all said as we hugged her.

Mom and Dad hugged us all and told us they would be up shortly to tuck us in. They were enjoying spending some time visiting with Grandma Linda. We all went up the stairs wishing each other goodnight as we went to our rooms. Gwenie showered first as I brushed my teeth and selected my school clothes for tomorrow. I showered, said my prayers and crawled into bed.

The phone rang. It was ringing our party line ring. Dad answered the phone and after a few minutes of silence I heard him tell someone he would go to his office and call them back in about half an hour. Dad came out of his room and walked downstairs. My brothers and sisters were all asleep in their beds. My bedroom is next to Mom and Dad's bedroom. Their bathroom is on the other side of my wall and then their bedroom with two walls of windows. I heard Mom turn the water off in her bathtub.

Dad had a phone added in their bedroom last week when the telephone man came. He had a long cord put on it so it would reach their entire room and bathroom. Mom was talking on the telephone. I could not hear every word clear so I went to my bathroom and picked up my water glass. I held it to my bedroom wall with my ear up against it. I could ear all of Mom's conversation perfectly.

"Oh Brenda, I feel so overwhelmed. Can you come?... Thursday would be perfect. Tim is bringing me all new butter papers on Wednesday for my order of one hundred pounds of butter Thursday. I have to bake bread and I need squares for the Kopple open house and then the party on Saturday at the hall. You, Bryan and the kids have to come to that as you will be neighbours soon. We have meeting in town on Friday. The county was here and they tested the dirt around. There are all kinds of different clays under the meadow in between our house and the road. They are going to use that clay to build your quarter mile road. They will leave us with a big shallow pond. They will put top soil back in so all the weeds and grasses will grow for the ducks and other birds… Can you believe Down Under is coming at two o'clock Sunday to sheer our sheep. Sunday or three weeks from now which is too late as the lambs will be coming. You know, I promised my niece and nephew they could help sheer sheep this year…Bryan defended Mr. Poffenroff in court after his wife was killed by that drunk driver just a mile from their home. Well, he is selling out his dairy. He sold all his Holstein cows. We bought his one Jersey, grain and all his little square bales of hay and straw that are coming Monday and Tuesday. Devon and Derek Nelson are trucking them in. We will help get them up in the loft. They are also going to start working with the twelve colts to break them......

Are your recliners defective? Well, our recliners, the Webster's and Grandma Linda's are defective. Every time we sit in them we fall asleep….That is just too funny. Anyway, Devon and Derek's Mother bought the last three that were damaged. They tore them all apart and covered the backs with calf hides so they had enough good leather left over to make those chairs look like new. I bet they are a treasure to behold… Absolutely, we have room for Daniel and Lily as well… That would be a blessing. I hope you are not too tired for your Thursday and Friday shifts next week… Are you still doing twelve hour shifts at the hospital or are they smart enough to put you back to eights?... Wow, tomorrow and Tuesday?... Okay, I will see you Thursday. Thank you Sis, I love you so much. Oh by the way, do you need to do any shopping at Webster's Western Wear? My little angels are wearing flood pants. I cannot believe how fast they are sprouting up. I definitely have to get them longer clothes. They seem to be so over worked. We haven't played games in ages. If they are not helping, they are sleeping… Okay, I will blame it on their needing more sleep as their bodies are growing and not us over working them… Oh, we been dealing with rustlers the last two days. They got four of our cows and thirty more from neighbours. They dumped them on Grandma Linda's far west quarter to hide until they thought it safe to transfer. Our cows started calling to the herd and they called back so we got them back… Can you believe we went to church and the kids could not remember their Bible verse for the first time ever? The only thing us adults can remember is being told to have an enjoyable Sunday. Can you image? Sitting through church and not absorbing one thing?... I don't think I could make this week without your help. We have a meeting tomorrow at Sheriff's office with all the other farmers that had rustled cattle… See you Thursday. Love you. Bye.

Wow, I cannot believe how busy this week is going to be for Mom. We are shearing our sheep this weekend. I love it. I think it might be a sin to eavesdrop, I am thinking. I knelt beside my bed, closed my eyes and folded my hands.

"Heavenly Father, please forgive me for using the glass so I could hear Mom's conversation on the phone to Aunt Brenda, her twin sister. Lord, I know sometimes Mom needs more help and if I know what is going on, I might be a better help to her. I know Dad does all he can to help, and he is a great cook. Lord, I promise not to gossip and I will not utter a word about my Aunt Brenda and Uncle Bryan building a home down the road. I am excited. Lord, help me to be a more helpful daughter, and a big help when our house is filled this weekend.

Sheering sheep is so much fun but a lot of work, too. Lord, please help me to be the best help and guide my footsteps and mouth so I can be your example of a caring, helpful sister they can look up to. Lord, bless us all and guide our mouths and footsteps to your honour. Lord, I guess it was wrong to listen through the glass, but I just want to know how I can best be a help, so thank you for forgiving me and please help me to be helpful. I ask this in Jesus name. Thank you for all my Blessings. Amen." I prayed.

I got off my knees and went to the window to check out the stars. The night was beautiful with a half moon and millions of stars twinkling. I heard Dad come up the stairs, as I stood at my window. I looked toward Grandma Linda's and didn't see any lights on at her house.

What is to the west? What is that orange light?

"Fire! Fire! Dad there is a fire," I screamed.

Watch for The Highwood Kids Book Two!

Treasure Life

Evan Ty Jenkins Pediatric Research Foundation

**Thank you for supporting the
Evan Ty Jenkins Pediatric Research Foundation
O/A Treasure Life.**

We are a registered non-profit in Alberta and a Federally registered charity in Canada dedicated to extending and improving quality of life for 1 in 100 children born with heart disease.

Your purchase of **The Highwood Kids** will assist us in delivering various programs in Edmonton hospitals including

Treasure Bead Program – All children admitted to the Stollery Childrens Hospital are eligible to participate in this program. Children receive an unique bead for each test or procedure they undergo and add them to a Treasure chain enabling them to document and talk about their medical journey. This highly successful program is also available in the NICU departments of the other three major Edmonton hospitals.

Medical equipment – Treasure Life purchases specialized equipment for Cardiac Kids to get them home sooner and safer. Purchases have now surpassed $400,000 and include such important equipment as coaguchek machines, oximeters, heart monitors, baby weigh scales, 4D portable echo machines, Tomtec specialized heart monitoring software and so on.

Treasure Logs – Many children suffering with congenital or acquired heart disease are subjected to many long days and often months of hospital stay. The Treasure logs are dual purpose, an activity book for the children and a section where the parents can keep important notes and dates about their child's stay in the hospital

www.treasurelife.ca

About The Author

LINDA HARRIMAN

Forty years of living the dream on paper

Raised in the foothills, I was born a cowgirl. Having worked in the lumber yard, on ranches, feedlots, dairy farms plus driving farm equipment and trucks, I have firsthand experience on living my life by the Code of the West with my Christian upbringing. This is the first novel of many as there is so much activity with these four siblings. Get lost in the pages of living and learning to be a cowboy or cowgirl. Come ride the range with me and experience the adventure of the West from the comfortable seat of your saddle.

www.thehighwoodkids.com
Email: thehighwoodkids@hotmail.com